Praise for *The Divorce Party*

"Events unfold over the course of a day, but the lessons learned have their roots in a lifetime." —*Elle*

"Elegant, accessible prose and compelling portraits of relationships, she has cultivated a star following." —*Cosmopolitan*

"You might think Dave would play this scenario for laughs, but she delivers plenty of poignant twinges." —*Newsday*

"Dave dives headfirst into the scary notion of sharing your life with someone, warts and all." —*Marie Claire*

"Insightful . . . *The Divorce Party* is a wry and observant novel about the relationship between an engaged woman and a woman on the verge of divorce, and the latter woman's divorce party." —*The Boston Globe*

"How well do you know the person you love? How hard would you fight if that relationship were threatened? Those questions lie at the heart of Laura Dave's *The Divorce Party* and the answers aren't as clear cut as one might think." —*San Francisco Chronicle*

"In lustrous, supple language and with breathtaking acuity, Laura Dave explores the intricate inner lives of two women as they struggle to know the men they love. . . . They face the same thorny question: how many lies—and how much truth—can love bear?" —Marisa de los Santos, author of *Love Walked In*

PENGUIN BOOKS

THE DIVORCE PARTY

Laura Dave is the author of the acclaimed novels *The Divorce Party* and *London Is the Best City in America*. Her writing has appeared in *The New York Times*, *Glamour*, *Self*, *Redbook*, *ESPN the Magazine*, and *The New York Observer*. Dave graduated from the University of Pennsylvania. In August, *Cosmopolitan* magazine named her as one of the eight "Fun and Fearless Phenoms" of 2008. She lives in California.

the divorce party

laura dave

PENGUIN BOOKS

PENGUIN BOOKS

Published by the Penguin Group

Penguin Group (USA) Inc., 375 Hudson Street, New York, New York 10014, U.S.A.
Penguin Group (Canada), 90 Eglinton Avenue East, Suite 700, Toronto,
Ontario, Canada M4P 2Y3 (a division of Pearson Penguin Canada Inc.)
Penguin Books Ltd, 80 Strand, London WC2R 0RL, England
Penguin Ireland, 25 St Stephen's Green, Dublin 2, Ireland (a division of Penguin Books Ltd)
Penguin Group (Australia), 250 Camberwell Road, Camberwell,
Victoria 3124, Australia (a division of Pearson Australia Group Pty Ltd)
Penguin Books India Pvt Ltd, 11 Community Centre, Panchsheel Park, New Delhi – 110 017, India
Penguin Group (NZ), 67 Apollo Drive, Rosedale, North Shore 0632,
New Zealand (a division of Pearson New Zealand Ltd)
Penguin Books (South Africa) (Pty) Ltd, 24 Sturdee Avenue,
Rosebank, Johannesburg 2196, South Africa

Penguin Books Ltd, Registered Offices:
80 Strand, London WC2R 0RL, England

First published in the United States of America by Viking Penguin,
a member of Penguin Group (USA) Inc. 2008
Published in Penguin Books 2009

1 3 5 7 9 10 8 6 4 2

Grateful acknowledgment is made for permission to reprint "Sweet Thing," words and music by Van
Morrison. © 1968 (renewed) WB Music Corp. and Caledonia Soul Music. All rights administered
by WB Music Corp. All rights reserved. Used by permission of Alfred Publishing Co., Inc.

PUBLISHER'S NOTE
This is a work of fiction. Names, characters, places, and incidents are either the product
of the author's imagination or are used fictitiously, and any resemblance to actual persons,
living or dead, business establishments, events, or locales is entirely coincidental.

THE LIBRARY OF CONGRESS HAS CATALOGED THE HARDCOVER EDITION AS FOLLOWS:
Dave, Laura.
The divorce party / Laura Dave.
p.   cm.
ISBN 978-0-670-01859-8 (hc.)
ISBN 978-0-14-311560-1 (pbk.)
1. Divorced people—Fiction.   I. Title.
PS3604.A938D58 2008
813'.6—dc22   2007040431

Printed in the United States of America
Set in Fairfield   Designed by Alissa Amell

When it falls, it falls all over you.

—Neil Young

the divorce
party

Montauk, New York, 1938

It is bizarre, of course, that this was the summer that everyone was trying to fly somewhere. Howard Hughes around the world in ninety-one hours, the luxurious Yankee Clipper boat off the water and into the air, Douglas "Wrong Way" Corrigan from New York to Los Angeles—he wound up in Ireland. It was also the summer after Superman first appeared in *Action Comics* and instant coffee got popular, and the last full summer before the worst war. But they'd talk about the flights first. They'd say, how odd, for everyone to have spent so much time staring up at the sky, and to still not see it coming: a hurricane so punishing that it would destroy America's eastern seaboard, biting off the farthest tip of eastern Long Island, biting off a town called Montauk, and leaving it detached from the world, an island, alone, in the middle of the ocean.

It was September, only the last vestiges of summer remaining, when the hurricane hit. No one on Long Island knew that a storm was coming that afternoon. That the army would have to come in to resurrect the land that had once connected Montauk to the rest of Long Island. That it would take two weeks before the waters receded low enough at Napeague to let through emergency traffic. That Montauk residents would lose almost everything.

In the end, there were only a few exceptions. Near Montauk Point, there were seven houses tucked so tightly to the bluffs that the wind and the rain and the water couldn't pull them down. Seven sister houses built by the same architecture firm in 1879, lived in each summer since by the same seven Manhattan families. Their steely gates and strong foundations completely intact. Their fireplaces and oak doors and stained-glass windows marking them, homes like trophies, on top of the end of the world.

The one at the farthest eastern tip was called Huntington Hall—Hunt Hall by anyone who'd actually visited. It was the only house of the seven still occupied that late in September. And occupying it was Champ Nathaniel Huntington.

Champ was thirty-three years old, and far too handsome, and a little too tall, and the only son of Bradley Huntington, the most successful publishing mogul in North America.

When the hurricane hit, Champ Huntington was having sex.

Lights on. Curtains drawn. Angry, late-afternoon sex. Anna was bent over the side of the bed, Champ behind her, his hand cupping her throat.

They had been out here all summer having sex like this. They were trying to save their marriage. And they were trying to destroy it.

Outside was all water and raging dark and storm. But in his faded consciousness, Champ didn't notice. He knew it was raining. He heard it striking against the roof. He heard the wind. But this was Montauk. It was September. These sounds didn't indicate that something brutal was happening.

Other things were brutal. This first year of marriage. It was wrong. Anna's dark hair in the sink. The meetings he didn't really have. He bent down farther, took her ear in his mouth.

"Don't," she said. She was focused, close. "Stop."

When they were done, they lay, splayed, Anna on the bed, Champ on the floor beneath her. Her foot was on his shoulder. This was the only place they were touching. He almost reached out, held her toes. But he knew it just made her mad when he did anything tender. It made her think he'd change, or want to try for her.

Then and only then did Champ sit up and look outside. And maybe it was that his head was still closed off, but what he saw out there looked like a train crashing into the window. It was the visual that made him hear the noise. The terrible whistling, high pitched and out of control. Hearing it, he'd later say, was the moment his life changed.

He headed to the bedroom window, naked, and had to reach out, grip the long edge of the window frame to hold himself up. He couldn't see the beach, or the ocean. He couldn't see anything at first.

Anna came up behind him, wrapped in the bedsheet, and they stood there watching the train-wind through the window. They watched so hard that they didn't talk. Not about the speed of the wind or the trees breaking apart or what must have been happening in the town center. If they had been thinking, they might have moved away from the window. They might have been scared that it would splinter. But they stood there until the storm stopped, and started, and stopped for good. And the greenish yellow sky turned purple and then black and the sun (or was it the moon?) rose up, terrifying. It was the sun. They had watched through the night.

"What time is it?" she asked.

He didn't answer her.

"What do we do now?" she said.

Champ was already in motion. He was putting on clothes and lacing up his work boots and walking out the front door. He made his way, by foot, across his land, down the slippery bluffs and tree-wrecked cliffs onto the flooded Napeague stretch and down farther to Main Street. Three and a half miles. Into the center of the ruined village.

There were fishing boats and cars piled on small houses. Fallen phone lines pulling down torn roofs. Poles and flooded cabinets and bed frames lining the street. Water was flowing from everywhere, making it hard to even walk down the streets—where did it start? If they figured out where it started maybe they could stop it!

Champ pulled up his pant legs and made his way to the Manor, where people were setting up shelter, where they were trying to provide relief for themselves. And Champ set to work with the other men moving cars and carrying wet wood and boarding windows and drying blankets and cleaning up slabs of broken glass.

How could he explain it even to himself? He didn't recognize the feeling, had never known it before. But something broke free in Champ—something like devotion or commitment—to his home, to his suffering town, to everything around him.

Maybe this is why, when he finished working, he didn't head home, but down to the docks, where he sat on canisters with all the fishermen, who now had nothing, and listened to them talk about how they had nothing, and stared at his own cut hands, and watched the moon rise, white and fierce, remarkably sure of itself.

Then he followed the star-line north and east, trying to locate it. First Montauk Point, then the cliff and the bluffs, then the house itself. His house. Huntington Hall. Standing tall, oblivious.

It was hard to find his way back there in the dark. So he followed the defeated shoreline, and eventually made his way up the wooden staircase, into the bluffs, toward his home, where everything was still mostly together. Where Anna was waiting with lit candles and tomato sandwiches, dark blankets spread out on the living room floor.

When he walked in, she was by the front door. She was wearing a long, purple sweater. She had her hair in a bun. She reached for him, and he buried into her neck, smelled her.

"How was town?" she asked, her hand still on his chest. "I tried to pick up news on the radio, but there was no reception. Is there a town left?"

He didn't answer her, but he was looking at her strangely. And he knew that she knew he was looking at her strangely. It was as simple as this: he could see her. For the first time in a year, there was nowhere else he was trying to be.

Which brought him to his own questions: Why did it take fear to move him? Why does it take chaos to make us understand exactly what we need to do?

He wanted to ask her his questions, but he wasn't sure she would have good answers, and then he would change his mind, and he didn't want to change his mind. He wanted to stay this sure.

Later, only thirty hours since he had last been lying there, they were lying on the floor together, facing each other. And in that strange way that we make decisions, the important decisions that ultimately make us, Champ decided that they were going to stay in Montauk full time. No more New York City. This had become their home.

He turned and looked outside at the slowly recovering world. At the backlit colors in the sky, on his lawn. And he knew the truth. The main truth, at least. This house had saved them. This big, beautiful cottage, which stayed big and beautiful despite the destruction all around. Its stern banisters and wood ceilings and determined rafters. The house had saved him, and he wasn't going to forget it.

He was going to build his life here, right here, in the name of love and honor and whatever else he was feeling, even if he couldn't name it for what it was: exhaustion.

He was, finally, exhausted.

He looked Anna right in the eye. "Things are going to be different," he said.

She nodded.

"I'm staying," he said, because they'd talked about the opposite, earlier, before—his leaving her, and here.

"Why?" she said.

"I want to," he said.

She got quiet. "You're going to disappoint me," she said.

"Probably." He was trying to make a joke, but it didn't come out that way. He tried again. "I think it's going to turn out okay," he said.

"Starting when?" she asked. "Ending when?"

Then, as if it were an answer, he pulled her in close to him, without reluctance, without anything like fear. "This house," he said, "will see love. This house will see everything."

part one

regrets only

Brooklyn, New York, 69 years later

Maggie

This is the truth, as far as she can see it: there are some things you should never talk about, and money is definitely one of them. Maggie is starting to understand this, in the way she often comes to understand the things that she wrongly believed she already had a handle on. No one wants to talk about money— whether you have very little or have a lot and feel slightly guilty about your lot in life, especially when it has been handed down to you, like bright red hair or childbearing hips, or the awful midnight disease that keeps its inheritors up all hours thinking about money and love and every other thing we, as human people, were never really meant to get to the bottom of.

Here's the point. Maggie doesn't sleep. Not since she and Nate moved to Red Hook, not since they plopped down every penny they have (and many that they don't have) into this fifteen-hundred-square-foot apartment, and—more critically— the two thousand square feet beneath it. The two thousand square feet that will be the home of their restaurant. She has never done anything like this—never made such a commitment to staying in one place. It isn't her strong suit. She knows this about herself—knows that a stranger would know this about her—just from looking at how she has organized her life: becoming a journalist, a food writer, straight out of college, living in eight cities in the eight years since. Spending time in well over thirty.

And while she really wants to open this restaurant—has dreamed of having a restaurant the entire time she has been writing about other people's—they don't go away all at once: money fears, fears of sitting still. She has thirty years of experience keeping those fears close to her. And now, in spite of herself, they are fighting to stay close, every time she tries to close her eyes.

So what does she do instead? She stares out the window. She plays her guitar. She reads Mediterranean cookbooks and waters the plants on the fire escape. She hums. She cleans. She imagines.

She thinks about Nate, lets the image of him in her mind wash over her, calm her. And though she has significant proof that her fiancé doesn't share her proclivity for sleeplessness—or endless worrying—she never suspected that he was so far on the other end of the money spectrum from her until now, when she comes across a pile of envelopes marked CHAMP NATHANIEL HUNTINGTON, in the middle of tonight's extensive, very unsatisfying cleaning spree.

Gross. It's gross to talk about money. But try to imagine. Maggie is sitting cross-legged in a white tank top and her Hello Kitty underwear in the middle of the living room floor surrounded by every paper and newspaper and old file and receipt and tax return that she could get her hands on. She is throwing it out, all of it out, and listening to Neil Young's *Harvest* on the record player and feeling like she is getting somewhere with her life. She is learning this is another side effect of her newfound insomnia: you often feel like you are getting somewhere with your life, until you rub your eyes, force yourself to focus, and realize you aren't far from where you started.

Maggie takes a deep stretch and reaches two feet in front of her, and there they are: a pile of envelopes with the CITIGROUP SMITH BARNEY logo on the front addressed to Champ Nathaniel Huntington. She removes the rubber band holding them together, and gets ready to open the first envelope. It doesn't occur to her to do otherwise. She isn't looking for information. She is looking for the opposite of information. She wants to find out that the Citigroup stuff is junk mail, and add the envelopes to her third filled garbage bag of recycling. And then she wants to take those bags and toss them into the alley behind Pioneer Street, into the hippo-sized trash cans waiting there for the New York City Department of Sanitation to take away.

This is the goal—to have their apartment in something like working order before they leave for Nate's parents' place out in Montauk later today, before they leave for his parents' for a reason she doesn't even want to think about, one she has been trying to avoid thinking about.

Nate's parents' divorce party.

Over the last several weeks—since she found out that they were going home to see Nate's family, since she found out *why* they were going—she's been tripping up, referring to it in her own head as an anniversary party. How could she not? A divorce party? What does this even mean?

Back in North Carolina, the closest she came to a divorce party was Loretta Pitt throwing Henry Pitt's things out of their third-floor bedroom window. Clothes and hats and dress shoes falling like snowflakes, like bricks. To music. Madonna, if Maggie's remembering. *The Immaculate Collection.*

But according to the tasteful green and white invitation her future in-laws sent them—according to the half dozen books that Nate's mom, Gwyn, sent along with it, named things like *A Graceful Divorce*—a divorce party is an important and necessary rite of passage, an important and necessary way to celebrate *a peaceful end to a valued union*. Her future in-laws just happen to be peacefully ending theirs on the very day Maggie is meeting them for the first time.

Fabulous.

The only good news is that knowing this is what she is headed to puts a new fire in her belly to get her own house in order. (Who is she kidding? Not wanting to come back to an apartment that is even messier than it was *before* she started cleaning it is putting a new fire in her belly.) But just as she is tearing open the first Champ Nathaniel Huntington envelope, she turns to see Nate standing in the living room doorway.

"What are you doing?" he asks.

He is wearing a pair of boxer shorts, no T-shirt. Dark hair standing on top of his head. Green eyes shining at her. Yawning. It is only 8 A.M., and Nate was downstairs breaking apart walls with the contractor—Johnson the Contractor, as they call him, as Johnson calls himself—until well after 5 A.M.

"What am I doing?" she asks. "What are *you* doing? Why are you up already?"

He shrugs, starting to stretch. "I can't sleep, I guess," he says.

Can't sleep? Nate can never *not* sleep. But here he is, walking barefoot across the floor, like proof that she is wrong, until he is standing directly above her. She follows his gaze as he checks out her endless piles of papers and newspapers, wrapped glasses and packs of wire hangers. She points to the open Fantastic bottle by her feet. She hadn't used it yet, but it is there.

"What?" she says. "I'm cleaning."

"I can tell," he says. He smiles his smile, the one that goes all the way to each ear, opening up his whole face, making him look younger and older at once. The first time she saw it, he was across the table from her at a farmer's market in the Ferry Building in downtown San Francisco. They were both searching through a pile of heirloom tomatoes. Dozens of tomatoes. He picked up a large yellow one with thin black ridges, smiled, and tossed it across the table to her. Somehow, she managed to catch it. *That's the best one there is,* he said.

And what were you going to say if I'd dropped it? she asked.

He looked down at the table, looked at all the tomatoes left. *I had about forty-nine more chances,* he said, *for things to go my way.*

"Maggie," he says now, gingerly pushing her piles out of the way, as if they were truly piles, and sitting down across from her, so that their knees are touching, so that his hands are holding her bare thighs.

"What?"

"Please tell me you haven't been doing this all night," he says.

"Why? Someone has to."

"Yes, but . . ." He wipes something off her face, maybe newspaper markings, maybe ink or dirt. "Hopefully someone who is actually getting somewhere with it."

Maggie looks away from him, tries to stop her face from turning red. He isn't making fun of her—or he is, but only because he wants her to make fun of herself. She can't, though, not exactly. She still harbors this idea, in the small place inside of herself that justifies her *Real Simple* subscription and the $250.00-plus tax she paid for her Bissel Healthy Home super-vacuum, that one day she will become the type of woman who is good at making things neat, beautiful, brand new.

She is good at other things—has already organized the entire computer and accounting system for the restaurant; feels more than confident about her ability to manage the front room once they open, her ability to run the bar.

But as fate would have it, she is marrying a man who has in him more of the woman she wants to be than she ever will. Nate is the best cook she has ever known, a natural cleaner, a builder. He keeps jars of fresh herbs on the kitchen counter. He carved their ratty rafters into a dining room table. He makes everything he touches beautiful. Even—though Maggie never imagined she'd feel this way—her.

She moves onto Nate's lap, wrapping her legs around his waist, her hand reaching around to rub his back. He is sticky, sticky from sleep and last night's sweat. She doesn't care. She could live like this. She smiles, and kisses him—his soft bottom lip, meeting hers, holding her there.

"What were you thinking about that you couldn't sleep?" she asks him. "How you don't want to marry me because I can't clean?"

"I want to marry you more because you can't clean."

"Terrible liar," she says.

"Terrible cleaner," he says.

He buries into her neck until she feels his smile press against her, his hands making his way under her panties—which is when she looks down at the floor, and her eyes catch them again. The pile of CITIGROUP SMITH BARNEY envelopes. The ones addressed to Champ Nathaniel Huntington.

"Hey, Nate," she says, over his shoulder. "Who is Champ Huntington, by the way?"

As soon as the words are out, she feels his body stiffen. And when he pulls back from her, slightly, she sees a bad look—one she doesn't recognize—come over his face.

"What did you just ask me?"

She reaches for the envelopes and hands them to him. "I just found these. Are they yours? Are they bank statements or something? I didn't know we had a bank account there. Do we?"

He looks down at the envelopes, flips them over in his hand, and nods. "Kind of."

This makes sense to her. They have "kind of" accounts open all over the city now, different accounts from many different institutions—lending them too little money at too high interest, all for the restaurant. Eight out of ten restaurants fail within the first year. Six out of ten marriages fail sometime after that. They are playing with some dangerous odds, if she lets herself think of any of this as playing. She tries not to.

"But who's Champ?"

He looks from the envelopes, up at Maggie's face. "I am," he says.

She starts to laugh, assuming that he is kidding. "Okay. Something you forgot to tell me about, Sport? I mean *Champ*?"

He smiles, but it is a nervous smile, and he doesn't say anything. He puts the envelopes down.

"Wait, you're serious? Your name is Champ?"

"No, my grandfather's name is Champ. Or was Champ. And I was named after him, but I've never used his name a day in my life. No one's ever called me Champ, but it is my official birth name. Champ Nathaniel Huntington."

Maggie knew that Nate was named after his grandfather, the one on his father's side, but she assumed that his name was Nate. She assumed it because Nate never told her otherwise.

"How have you never mentioned that?" she asks.

He shrugs. "Would you want to mention that?"

It isn't a bad point. But, inadvertently, she must make a face because Nate looks pretty nervous.

"Wow," he says, "you're never going to have sex with me again, are you? Who would? Who would have sex with someone named Champ?"

She starts to laugh, and grabs the back of his neck, holds him. He is blushing—Nate, Champ, whoever—really blushing. And it makes Maggie feel bad that she mentioned the envelopes.

"It has nothing to do with you. I just don't think it was very nice of your parents, that's all," she says, making him meet her eyes. "Or your grandfather's parents . . ."

Nate nods, putting the envelopes down. "No kidding," he says. He looks at Maggie in a way she does recognize—in a way that tells her he needs to say something that is hard for him to say. "But I think that's why I couldn't really sleep."

"What?" she says. "You thought someone would call you Champ and blow your cover?"

But he isn't laughing. "Truthfully? I'm a little nervous for you to meet my family."

"Why? Because of the divorce?"

She looks at him carefully, his sweet and handsome face. She reaches out to touch it with the back of her fingers. She would understand if he was nervous for her to meet his parents because of their impending divorce, but he keeps insisting that he is okay with it. He keeps insisting that his parents have just had *a parting of ways* since his father decided he wanted to convert to Buddhism and started moving his life in that direction. He keeps insisting that his parents, together, decided this meant their lives were going in very different directions. After thirty-five years together. *How can Nate be so okay with that?* Maggie's wondered to herself more than once. Isn't it the point of marriage—Maggie can't make herself ask out loud—that you figure out how to make the different directions meet?

"There are just things," he says, "important things that you should know before we go. Things that I probably should have told you before now."

She tries to figure out how to say it so he hears her. "Nate, they could have three heads, and it wouldn't change anything. I don't care," she says.

And she doesn't. Historically, she would have. But historically she has been the one in any relationship looking for the way out. It used to take less than half a reason for her to look for an exit: someone's parents, someone's use of cologne, someone's affection for Sting. But with Nate it is different, has been different from the beginning.

"Like what?" she says. "Your parents are actually going to stay married?" She is joking around, but he isn't biting.

"I'm not sure you're ready to hear."

"I'm ready to hear," she says. "Of course I'm ready to hear. Do I need to remind you that my childhood was not *Leave It to Beaver*?"

And it wasn't. Unless you consider being raised alone by a less-than-fully-grown-up bar and grill owner in Asheville, North Carolina, *Leave It to Beaver*. Unless you consider Eli Mackenzie's well-intentioned, but ill-advised choices—like having his fifteen-year-old daughter help with midnight shifts at the bar so they could have more time together—idyllic.

Nate smiles. "Wasn't *Leave It to Beaver* a little before your time?"

Nate is four years older than Maggie is. He likes to pretend

he is ten years older. Or, when it serves his purposes, a hundred.
"Just tell me," she says.

"You sure?"

"No time like the present."

But then she puts her nose to his neck—and a heavy smell,
like a swirling heat, like a combination of salmon and bad milk,
comes back at her. "Jeez. What on earth is that smell? Do I even
want to know?"

"Not good?" he says.

"No." She shakes her head. "Not good."

"That is Johnson the Contractor's homemade one-hundred-
herb gel. Complete with garlic extract and dried fish flakes from
a sorcerer in Chinatown. He carries around a huge jelly jar of
the stuff, and swears that it will relieve any residual pain I feel
from last night's labor."

"Well, I hope it does, but . . . yuck," she says, and for some
reason, moves in closer to get a more pungent whiff. "That is one
of the worst things I've ever smelled. You are maybe one of the
worst things I've ever smelled."

"That may be good news."

"How do you figure?"

"Because when you move away from me when I tell you this
next thing I'm going to tell you, I can blame it on the gel."

"I'm ready," she says, covering her eyes, in an exaggerated
fashion, pretending that she is bracing herself, as if for a doctor's
needle shot, flinching in anticipation.

"It's about my family's money situation. It's about what you
would have found out if you opened those envelopes."

She uncovers her eyes, meets his. She feels herself breathe
out, feeling terrible that this is what he's worried about. She has
already made the assumption that while Nate's family may be

fairly comfortable—his father a pediatrician, his mother a former art teacher—they are certainly not very comfortable, considering that even with the restaurant's silent investor, even with Eli giving them a little help, Maggie and Nate have been scrimping and saving and scrimping more, and taking out loans from three banks starting with the letter W and two different ones starting with C. Apparently, actually, three banks that start with C.

But maybe she was wrong to assume that Gwyn and Thomas were even fairly comfortable. Even if Nate did grow up out in Montauk. Maybe she was wrong to assume.

"I don't care about that, Nate," she says. "How can you think I'd care about that? Your family's money situation . . . it makes no difference to me."

"Really?"

She nods. "I promise you."

"Good," he says, putting his mouth on her forehead. "Because my family has close to half a billion dollars."

Gwyn

There are rumors, you know. There are always rumors. Rumors that people take as truth without ever getting to it.

You know, what the actual story is.

This bothers Gwyn. Rumors, half-truths. Like: with the cake, just as an example. The red velvet cake. The rumor with the red velvet cake is that it was invented—that the first one was made—at the restaurant in the Waldorf-Astoria Hotel in New York City in the early 1900s. The story goes that the pastry chef there made a cake one night using red dye, and a hotel guest liked the cake so much that she asked for the recipe, only to find out at checkout that she had been billed several hundred dollars for it. When she tried to complain, the hotel refused to remove the charge. Looking to get even, she spread the recipe to all her friends, all over the country. And all her friends forwarded it on to all of their friends. . . .

The point is that it's a charming story, but it's crap. Gwyn knows this. She knows the real story of the red velvet cake, its real history, is less like a fun rumor and more like a warning. The real story, about most things, in Gwyn's recent experience, is often more like a warning.

Of how things go wrong.

Of how they go.

She sighs—she is not normally a sigher, but she sighs—thinking about it. Then she checks the car clock: 9:15 A.M. Gwyn has been sitting here for a half hour already, in the small parking lot at the East Hampton airport, in her red Volvo wagon. Thomas was supposed to have landed by now. But, of course, he hasn't. At these small airports, you can't count on things to go as planned. And besides, Gwyn should be blaming herself, if anyone. She is the one who organized it so that Thomas would get back from his medical conference the morning of their party. It took quite a bit of finagling, in fact, to orchestrate it this way: an overnight flight from LAX to JFK; a second private flight out here. She wanted—no, she needed—Thomas to get back now, this late in the game, so she would know what to do with him, how to keep him busy, so that her plans for tonight stayed in motion, without disruption, exactly as she planned them.

She isn't confident, though. Not about any of it going the way she needs it to. Except for the cake. She is confident about the cake. Because she is good at making it, and because it is Thomas's favorite. It is his favorite thing that she makes for him. It was the first thing she ever made for him: their first date, the two of them sitting on the roof of her building in New York City. The only building she ever lived in in the city, on Riverside Drive. The best thing that it had going for it was its proximity to Columbia (where she had been enrolled at the Teachers College), and its roof—the piece of the river that the roof looked out over. Thomas brought a bottle of wine with him—a 1945 Château Mouton-Rothschild. And they sat on the roof until 2 A.M., eating the red velvet cake, sharing sips of the wine straight from the bottle.

Of course, the wine could have been from the corner deli for all she knew. She didn't have any idea then that the wine was worth thousands and thousands of dollars. (Thomas didn't either. He just grabbed a bottle from his father's wine cellar before heading in to the city to see her.) Especially, at twenty-two, she wouldn't have agreed to drink it if she had known.

But Gwyn knew the most important thing that first night, even if she hadn't wanted to. Thomas got the last piece of cake. There was the sweet arguing back and forth—*you take it, no you take it*—but Thomas got it. It makes it fitting, then, that he will get the last piece now too.

Her phone rings, loud, too loud, even from the bottom of her bag. She searches for it, hoping it is Eve. Let it be Eve. This is the woman Gwyn has hired to cater tonight's party. Eve Stone of Eve's Kitchen. Quogue, New York.

Gwyn has been trying to reach her, all morning, to no avail, and all she can think is that she has no idea how to do this.

She has no idea how to plan this divorce party tonight. She has been to a few divorce parties. And there are plenty of books she's found that encourage the idea of having a healing divorce, of celebrating it—*Filing Is Not Failing; The Last Dance You Can Dance; Good-bye Can Be Another Word for Hello!* But they are for people who aren't secretly laughing at the idea of a divorce party, people who buy into something Gwyn is only pretending to buy into.

That things can end well.

That things can—just—end.

She flips open her phone right after the fourth ring. "Eve?" she says. "Is that you?"

"Who's Eve? No, Mom. It's me."

Me is Georgia. Gwyn's daughter. Gwyn's daughter who has

no idea what is really happening with her parents. Not her daughter, not her son. Yes, they know their parents are getting divorced. She has been trying to shield them from the rest. Or, at least, this is what she's told herself. But maybe her motives aren't as pure as that. Maybe she hasn't told them everything because, once she does, there is no going back. Once she's said the words out loud, about what's really going on, she can't decide to believe something else.

"What's going on, sweetheart?" Gwyn asks, adjusting the phone in her hand. "Is everything okay?"

"Define 'okay.'"

"Are you in labor?"

"Not that I'm aware of."

"Good." Gwyn nods. "That's good."

That is good. Even if Gwyn knows that Georgia gets annoyed every time she asks, it is a relief to her. Georgia has been in from L.A., staying with Gwyn for the last couple of weeks while her French boyfriend, Denis (pronounced, as Georgia loved to remind them, as if they've ever gotten it wrong, Den-*eè*), has been making a record with his band in Omaha, Nebraska. Twenty-five-year-old Georgia, who is eight and a half months pregnant. Eight and a half months pregnant with the baby of a man she has known for ten and a half months. Not the wisest course of action, if anyone asked Gwyn's opinion on the matter. But no one did.

No one asked her opinion on Maggie either. Maggie, who Gwyn has only talked to on the phone, but who has a laugh that Gwyn likes, a laugh that Gwyn trusts, especially because she has learned, over time, that the way someone laughs often mirrors who they are. How they are. Maggie's laugh is empathetic, giving. She'll take either of those qualities for Nate. She'll gladly take both.

"Mom."

"Georgia."

"Did Dad's plane land yet? I need to talk to him. Denis cut his hand on a corkscrew and he doesn't want to get on a plane to come here if there is something really wrong with it. If he needs to go to a hospital in Omaha or something. It's his left hand. He needs it to work properly. He is the bass player."

"What if he was the drummer? Would it not matter then?"

"Mom, please be serious. I need Daddy to tell Denis what to do."

Daddy. Georgia still looks to him to tell her what to do, still finds it easy to be his child. Will it be the same with Denis and Georgia's kid—the love with the father easier, longer? Why does it always seem to go that way? The love going to the one who is around a little less, and therefore seems to deserve it a little more?

"I'll have him call you."

"Thank you," she says. And then, as if something occurred to her, her voice gets louder. "Oh, and will you also tell him that that woman from the meditation center called the house again? I couldn't understand exactly what she was saying, but she wants Dad to call her. She said his cell phone isn't working. She said that he would know what she was calling about."

Gwyn feels her heart seize. Another call for Thomas. From the meditation center. How on earth did they get here? Gwyn is the daughter of a southern minister—a southern minister who heads a congregation near Savannah, Georgia, of twenty-five hundred people. And for the first several years of their marriage she could barely get Thomas to go home with her for Easter, for Christmas. He would agree, grudgingly, only after saying that it made him feel like a hypocrite. To pretend to believe. He is a doctor, a man of science. This is where he is placing his bets. *It doesn't have to be one or the other,* she used to tell him.

Yes, he would say. *It does.*

But then, nine months ago, he came home from teaching his weekly seminar on health care reform at Southampton College and told Gwyn that he was thinking more about spirituality. Eastern spirituality. He told her that he would be staying at the college late on Mondays to take a class in Buddhist Thought, that he would be driving down to Oyster Bay to attend meditation classes on Thursday mornings. That he would be driving all the way into Manhattan for weekend-long retreats at the Chakrasambara Buddhist Center. Where he couldn't be reached for three days at a time.

I just want to see, he said.

Until he wanted to do more than just see, which was when the real problems started.

I think my life is going in a different direction, he said, casually, over dinner one night—over sautéed bluefish; a small lentil salad—as if he had changed his mind about wanting these things for dinner, as if it were of no real consequence either way.

It feels unclear to me right now where it fits into that, he said. *You know . . .*

No, Thomas, she said. *I don't know.*

Our marriage.

Gwyn looks at herself in the rearview mirror, the phone still against her ear. She is symmetrical. This is the nicest thing she can think about herself right now. The rest of it—the long, blond hair, matching long legs; her cool blue eyes and still fairly lovely skin; *her beauty*—it has deceived her. In its own way, it has made her feel secure. For fifty-eight years, her beauty has made her feel safe. In her marriage, in her family, in her own skin. But she hasn't been. Her husband is acting like someone she doesn't know. Her son never wants to come home. Her daughter never wants to leave.

She is the opposite of safe. And this is the secret she wants to tell, if anyone wants to hear, this is what she wants to warn people of: Beauty won't protect you. Not in the end. What will is the one thing you can't plan for. The one thing you can't save for or search for or even find. It has to find you and decide to stay. Time. More of it. More of it to try and make things right. As of today, Gwyn is just about out.

"Mom," Georgia says. "Are you listening to me? Who is Eve?"

"What?"

"Eve? You asked me when I got on the phone if I was Eve. Who is she?"

Gwyn looks toward the landing strip in the distance, as if she were about to get caught. For what, and by whom, she can't say. But a plane has landed in the time since Georgia called, a small jet plane hitting the tarmac, coming to a complete stop. This too she has missed.

"Eve is the caterer," she tells Georgia. "She is catering tonight's party for us. She hasn't called the house, has she?"

"No, what do you need from her if she does?"

"Everything," Gwyn says.

Georgia laughs. This is funny? Apparently this is funny. Apparently, Gwyn has made a joke.

"Sweetheart, I'll call when Dad gets here, okay? I'll ask him about Denis's hand and I'll have him call you. But I've got to jump off now."

"Why?"

How can she answer? She doesn't want to. She doesn't want to go into any of it with Georgia, not now, not without telling her the whole story. But what is the whole story? Part of it, at least, starts to tell itself because there is a knock on the window, a loud knock, which Georgia surely hears through the phone. And Gwyn looks out to see a young guy, standing there—post-college, clean shaven, a little too tan. Her guy. The messenger. And he is carrying a briefcase, a metal briefcase, the temperature inside regulated, controlled.

Gwyn's briefcase.

She rolls down her Volvo's window to greet him, manually rolls it down. The Volvo is more than fifteen years old, and requires the turning of an actual lever. Gwyn doesn't mind, likes it actually, as it gives her a second to compose herself. Because when the window is down, the messenger gives her a big smile, a smile she is used to getting from men she is just meeting, a smile of approval. These days, such smiles unnerve her. They remind her she may have to start paying attention to them again.

"Mrs. Huntington?" he asks.

"Yes?"

"I'm Peter Blevins from the winery," he says. "My apologies that the flight was delayed."

"No reason to apologize. You weren't flying the plane, were you?"

Peter seems to appreciate this, coming from her. "If I were, I would have been more effectual."

Effectual? The word surprises her coming out of his mouth, continues to surprise her as he hands over his card, proof that he is who he says he is. He opens the briefcase and takes out the bottle of wine she ordered. The bottle of wine that he flew across the ocean to hand-deliver for Gwyn and Thomas's party this evening. A bottle of 1945 Château Mouton-Rothschild.

"I'm glad to open it for you," he says, "so you can make sure that it is to your liking."

"I'm sure it's fine."

"I've been instructed to open it," he says, and looks worried.

"Well," she says, more firmly, "I'm changing the instructions."

He nods, and Gwyn wonders how many people check a $26,000 bottle of wine to make sure it has aged appropriately. Especially one flown in on a private plane from across the Atlantic.

"Mr. Marshall sends his loving regards," he says.

Look at that, she thinks. What treatment! For $26,000 plus the cost of the messenger's flight, you don't just get a bottle of wine, but regards, loving regards, from someone you don't know.

"Please send him my best as well," she says.

Through the cell phone, she hears her daughter, screaming: "Mom! Did I just hear that you flew in wine? You've got to be kidding me. That's what you are at the airport picking up?"

"That's what I'm picking up," she says, and rolls up the window. "It's for the toast tonight."

"Have you lost your mind?"

Gwyn thinks about this, as she tucks the briefcase under the seat. "Yes. I think I may have."

"What about Dad, Mom?"

"I have to get home, and bake the cake."

"But who is picking up Dad?"

Who is picking up Dad? This isn't what Gwyn wants to talk

about. If anything, she wants to talk about the cake. The real story behind the red velvet cake. The first baker to make it—a southern woman, from a town less than fifty miles from where Gwyn grew up—wanted to make a cake that meant something, that symbolized the contrast between good and evil: the good represented by the lily white frosting, the evil represented by the red colored cake. The baker had thought that even if it didn't taste so different from other chocolate cakes, people would decide it tasted different. Because it had it all in there. Good and evil. Holy and unholy. Right and wrong. And she was right, wasn't she? People are drawn to the cake even if they have no idea why. They have no idea that they are counting on it. You know, to save them.

Does her daughter want to hear about that? No, she doesn't think so. She doesn't think she is ready.

"Mom," Georgia says again. "Who is getting Dad?"

"Your father is effectual," she says.

"What does that have to do with anything?"

Gwyn turns on the ignition. "He can take a cab."

Maggie

They've been standing on the corner of Forty-first and Third, in front of the Au Bon Pain, waiting for the Hampton Jitney to pick them up. They've been standing here for twenty minutes, and Maggie keeps staring at her fingernails, occasionally biting on one, as if that is actually an all-consuming activity, as if this leaves her no energy for anything else. She has no energy for anything else. She doesn't want to look at Nate and she doesn't want to look at the guy in the suit standing on the other side of her either. The guy is on his cell phone and typing on his Black-Berry at the same time. He also keeps looking at Maggie's ass. Your regular multitasker.

When he catches Maggie's eyes, he winks at her and mouths, "Do you belong to him?" About Nate. Nate is looking down, and doesn't notice. But this makes her reach for him, hold his arm.

It is the first time she's reached for him since they've been back at the apartment, since his big announcement, which is probably why Nate turns to her, a little hopeful, adjusting his backpack higher on his shoulder. "Do you think it's going to rain?"

"What?"

He points up at the sky, which is blue and cloudless. "It looks like it's going to, doesn't it?"

"That's what you want to talk about, Nate?"

"No, it's not what I want to talk about. But I thought it might be a start."

Maggie isn't sure what to say. Her head is hurting, throbbing actually, a combination of being absolutely exhausted and being unable to wrap her mind around what Nate has told her—half a *billion* dollars; what does that even mean? What does that look like? And why did he say half a billion as opposed to, say, five hundred million? Does he think it makes it sound smaller, to cut it in half?

She has no idea. But what she actually feels mad about— what she can wrap her head around—is that, if she had known, she would have packed differently. Not that she has some fancy clothing hiding in the bottom of their closet, in the bottom of their unpacked boxes. But maybe she would have found something. Her grandma's ruby ring or her one black cashmere sweater. Yes, it's September, and, *yes,* it's probably too early for cashmere. But if she had had more time to think, she would have grabbed it, put it in her bag, or just draped it around her shoulders. Something. Maybe, at the very least, she would have become the kind of person who knows whether it is too early for cashmere.

"So . . ." Nate runs his fingers through his hair, messing it up. "I'm trying to give you space, but if you're not careful, we're going to get all the way to Montauk, and we still won't be past this. That will be worse."

"Says who, Champ?"

He moves in closer, putting his arms around her, bending so he is looking her in the eyes. "I like it when you get passive aggressive, and pissed off," he says. "You look like your first-grade picture."

"Great. I'm glad this is fun for you." But she is starting to smile as she says it.

"The money thing isn't really a big deal," he says. "You probably wouldn't have even known unless I told you. Or, you'd know they have some money, but not how much. I guess once I admitted it, I just kept going."

"So you admit it?"

"What?"

"That there was something to admit?"

He shakes his head, takes an exaggerated breath as if he is trying to find the words. "People with a lot of . . . They are the opposite of people with some. They do the opposite of showing it. My mom doesn't even have an engagement ring, just her wedding band. They drive fifteen-year-old cars."

"And they have divorce parties."

"The divorce party didn't bother you when you didn't know about the money."

"Because I thought it was something I just didn't know about yet. But now it's starting to feel like something I don't want to know about. Like debutante balls or . . . I don't know . . . boarding schools in Switzerland for advanced six-year-olds."

He ignores her, which is wise right then. "The reason that I told you about my family's financial situation is that I didn't want you to walk into their house and feel sideswiped."

"Right, but finding out an hour *before* I meet them couldn't possibly have the same effect."

"The bus ride is actually closer to three hours."

"Very funny."

"No. It's not. By the second hour, it's not funny at all. Nause-ating, a little. But not exactly funny."

She looks at him and feels something in her soften. She starts to smile, smiles because he is. She smiles because he, as usual, is looking at her until she does. He is looking at her like she is the only thing he really cares to see.

"Nate, I'm not trying to make a big deal. But wouldn't you be a little freaked out too? If the situation was reversed? I mean, you say *people with money*. But it's not people. It's your people, your family. It just feels like a big thing to not have known about you all this time, especially with all the conversations we've been having about finances because of the restaurant."

She doesn't know how to explain it exactly, even to herself, except that she thought Nate had told her everything about himself. She thought they both had told each other everything. It isn't as much about the money, but that *that* has turned out to be wrong. He knows everything about her. Every terrible, boring thing that it wasn't her instinct to share. That he—in his way—encouraged her to share. Now she wonders what else she doesn't know about him.

"But that's the thing. It isn't about me. It's my grandfather's money, or his grandfather's money. I haven't touched any of it since I left home. I made that decision a long time ago. I even paid for school myself. You know that."

She does know that. He mentioned it when they figured out that they both went to the University of Virginia—same small-town campus—Nate two years ahead of Maggie; two years ahead of her after his two years off—though they never met there. She thinks of her own loans, $1,100 that she needed to pay to a woman named Sallie Mae by the fifth of each month on a traveling food critic's salary, the $1,100 she still needs to pay to Sallie Mae each month.

"Well, that was just stupid of you," she says.

He puts his head to her head as if to say, *thank you*. Thank you for making a joke, for laughing. For letting us be us. She reaches for his ear, tugs at it, thinks of him at UVA, and how remarkable it is that they could have met almost a decade before they did. She has a few distinct memories now of seeing him there—on the other side of the student union one rainy Sunday morning, using the Sunday paper to try to dry off his arms; at a basketball game sitting in the last row of the visiting team's side with friends, wearing a bright-red UVA sweatshirt. They are so vivid, the memories, but how can she really know if they are real or imaginary? How can she know which way is better?

He leans down, talks into her hair. "Can I tell you something I've never told you before?" He pauses. "I like you more than anyone."

She looks up at him. This is what Nate always says to her— what they always say to each other—instead of *I love you*, instead of *I'll never leave*. I like you the most, like a promise: I want you, and I always will.

"I like you more than anyone, too," Maggie says.

Then—before she has to take another look at their Black-Berry friend, before she has to think about any of the rest of it—a bus is pulling up with large green paneling on the side, HAMPTON JITNEY written in white letters. They get in line, head onto the bus, behind an older couple who is bickering with the driver about a surfboard: under the bus, over, under.

The first several rows are already filled with passengers from previous stops. As they pass row three, Maggie catches the eye

of a woman sitting there—exotic more than pretty, and strikingly thin—who looks at Nate, really looks at him, does a double
take as they walk by. Nate doesn't seem to notice, but Maggie
does. She is still not used to this, how women look at Nate. At
first, she kind of liked it. But now she doesn't care if anyone else
thinks Nate is attractive, especially because their looks feel so
predatory. As if how he looks is all they see. As if any of his
more human qualities, or the fact that he isn't looking back, can
be made untrue, invisible.

In the first free aisle, Maggie squeezes into the window seat,
Nate shoving their belongings in the rack above their heads before taking the aisle seat, handing her a brown bag.

"What's in there?" she asks.

"Your favorite."

"My favorite?" she says, peeking inside.

But she knows what it is, before she even looks. Nate has
made her his famous peanut butter popcorn concoction: popcorn with homemade peanut butter sauce and a variety of salty
and sweet herbs. It may sound disgusting, especially in the
morning, but it is Maggie's ultimate comfort food. And, with all
the fancy, wonderful things Nate can cook so well, she still
loves this the most.

"When did you have time to do this?"

He leans over and kisses her on the cheek. "It's amazing
what I can get done when you refuse to speak to me."

Maggie smiles. "Ha ha," she says, and takes a bite, then another bite, breathing in the secret ingredient (coconut) and starting to feel better. Immediately and completely better.

This is going to be fine. All of it will be fine. The reason he
didn't tell her until now about the money is that it wasn't important to him. It wasn't a part of him, and therefore of them either.

It had nothing to do with them. Nothing is different. They will go see his parents, like they planned, go to their bizarre party, and head back to New York, to their restaurant at the tip of Brooklyn. Twenty-four hours from now, and this will be behind them.

"Good?" he says.

"Very good," she says. "Thank you."

"You're welcome."

She brushes his hair off of his face, moves closer to him, which is when she gets her next surprise. The model-like woman from the front of the bus is standing there. She is wearing a tiny green dress, bug-shaped glasses, and looks better from this angle—the thin turning into sculpted, the strikingly gaunt turning into simply striking—as if this were the angle, from below her, you're actually supposed to be watching her from.

"Nate Huntington," she says. "I thought it was you."

Nate looks flummoxed for a minute, and—as his eyes register the woman, he looks *more* flummoxed, as if he has just been caught in something. And from the way he is looking back and forth between Maggie and whoever this is, Maggie wonders what he thinks he is being caught for.

"Murphy . . ." Nate says, standing up and giving her a hug. "What a small world."

When Nate pulls back, Murphy—*Murphy?* really?—keeps her arms wrapped around his neck in a familiar way.

"Not that small, *mon ami*. Or it wouldn't have been so long since I last laid eyes on you."

Maggie puts her paper bag of popcorn down, trying to sit up taller at the same time, which makes the popcorn spill all over her lap and the seat. The good and bad news is that Nate and Murphy are talking so intensely, Maggie is able to brush it off before they notice.

"Murphy Buckley, this is Maggie Mackenzie. Maggie, this is Murphy, an old friend of mine from growing up."

"You can call me Murph," she says to Maggie, holding out her hand. "It's good to meet you. I saw you get on the bus. I noticed your shoes."

Does that mean she liked my shoes? Maggie looks down at her worn, gold ballet slippers and sincerely doubts it. Maggie instinctively tucks her legs beneath herself, and pulls her hair behind her ears. It is something she does when she is feeling nervous, tugging on her best feature, or what she thinks is her best feature—her long, dark hair—and really, combined with her dark eyes and skin, someone *could* make the argument that she, Maggie, is pretty. But, Maggie knows, someone could make the other argument too. Not like Murph. There is only one argument to make about her.

"Maggie and I are getting married," Nate says.

"Seriously? I don't believe it!" Murph says. "You are engaged? I didn't think that day would come. No judgment or anything. I keep saying I'm not done with marriage, and I've been married two and a half times at this point, but . . ."

Nate interrupts her—in a very un-Nate-like moment, as he doesn't usually interrupt people. It may be the first time, or at least the first time she remembers, that she has heard him interrupt anyone. But she can see something in his eyes when he does it—the defensiveness—that kicks up in Nate so rarely that it surprises her, unnerves her, to see it now.

"Murph and I grew up down the road from each other," he says. "Really next door to each other . . ." He makes a triangle sign with his hands, as if to show the location points of each of their houses—Murph at the thumbs, Nate at the index fingers. "We went to high school together."

"If you can call it high school," she says. "It wasn't exactly chock-full of homecoming dances or pep rallies. More like eleven of us sitting in my parents' living room every day with a private tutor because our parents deemed East Hampton High unworthy." She shines her shiny teeth at Maggie. "Not exactly hard to win most popular when my kitchen supplied the Diet Coke."

Maggie tries to catch Nate's eyes. Is that how half billionaires are educated?

"Maggie loves Diet Coke," Nate says.

Maggie nods because she knows this is his way of trying to include her, which ends up making her feel worse. That this is the best way he found: utilizing a soft drink.

"Who doesn't?" Murph says.

"Probably the people who make Diet Pepsi," Maggie says. She is surprised by the anger in her own voice, the edge beneath the joke, but Murph doesn't notice. Or at least Murph pretends not to notice, laughing loudly instead, her head flying back.

People are scrambling to pass her in the aisles, which makes Maggie hope that maybe Murph will just go back to her *own* seat, already. But she doesn't seem to notice the people who need to get by. Or maybe she just doesn't care.

"So I have a bone to pick with you, by the way . . ."

Guess she's staying.

"How could you just skip out on our reunion? Leave me alone with all those lunatics when you know it is *the end of me*?"

"I'm sorry about that. We were still out in California, and trying to get it together to move here."

"Excuses, excuses! We all had dinner at Soho House. Grayson came in from Boston and Lis and Marlo flew in from Dubai. And Bedlan Blumberg hosted the whole thing because, you know, he's so over trying to impress anyone. Yeah, right. Anyway . . . we drank like nine magnums of Veuve. I swear, I nearly passed out *at the table*. And, at three A.M., we are all totally hammered, and Buddy rises up to make a toast, and tells us that he has an announcement to make, and the announcement is that he is gay. We were like, Buddy, *no fucking kidding*. We've only known this our entire lives. But thanks for the tip, Jackass."

She pauses, breathes in. "It was a blast."

Nate starts to laugh, a little too loudly, and Maggie wonders if she missed something. It's possible. What had she and Nate discussed about their high schools? She can't remember now. Could it be so little that she has somehow incorrectly assumed that Nate's high school looked something like hers? One with a big gym and bad cafeteria food and an even worse football team? Or did he say something that made her think those things? She looks at him more carefully. What else did she assume that maybe she should remember to ask him about now? What else about the way he grew up is going to come into focus in the next twenty-four hours?

Murph is holding her hand over Nate's chest, over his heart. "So have I been hearing right? You are back from San Fran, for good, and opening this *very* big-deal restaurant?"

"I wouldn't jump to calling it a big deal, but, yes, we're opening a restaurant out in Brooklyn, Red Hook, actually," Nate says. And, thankfully, he steps back, so Murph has no choice but to let his chest go.

He shrugs at Maggie, as if to say, *I'm sorry*.

She shrugs back, as if to say, *it's okay*. But truthfully—if she's allowed to be truthful with herself—it doesn't feel okay, or at least, not exactly.

"Red Hook, huh?" Murph says. "I didn't know that anyone actually lived there. Wow! It's like you're an explorer."

"Something like that," Nate says.

"When is opening day?"

"Our soft opening is Halloween weekend. And, if all goes as planned, we want to be up and running in time for the holidays."

"That's exciting."

The person behind Murph in the aisle clears his throat loudly. Murph moves over, a drop, so he can almost squeeze past. When he waits for her to really move out of the way, when he gingerly coughs again so she will, she gives him a look as if to say, *up yours*.

"Well, I better head back up front. If I have to sit back here with you two, I'll get seasick, Captain."

Captain?

"We should hook up this weekend. Maybe get everyone together and head over to the Liars Saloon. Do a little drinking. Have a little fun. Old-school style. Wouldn't that be the greatest?"

Nate nods. "If we can get away. It's kind of a crazy weekend, and we're actually only here because . . ."

"Oh that's right! How could I forget? I heard that Gwyn and Thomas are having a divorce party tonight. I was surprised to hear they were splitting up, to tell you the truth. It's temporary, I'm sure, *I'm sure* . . . I'd be willing to bet you that it is." Then Murph turns toward Maggie. "Don't you just love Gwyn and Thomas? I mean, just look at them! Who is beautiful enough for either of them except the other?"

Maggie shakes her head. "I haven't met them yet actually. I've spoken to them on the phone many times, but this is the first time we'll be meeting in person." She can't stop talking, apparently. "Face to face . . . because we were in California, and they were here, and we've been setting up the restaurant . . . and they've been going through . . ."

Murph raises her eyebrows, as if to say, *who are you talking to, me or yourself?* And Maggie wishes she had a good answer, but the truth is she has been telling herself too loudly all the reasons Nate hasn't introduced her yet to his family. And now, she is wondering if she knows the real one.

"Well, anyway, you will love them," Murph says. "I remember every time I was over there, they would sit so near to each other on the couch, sharing a bowl of fruit or a glass of bourbon. I don't think I've ever seen my parents sit in the same room unless other people were there too. They are the ones who should be getting divorced, but I think my mother is too tired to house hunt." She pauses, shaking her head. "But Gwyn and Thomas were, year after year, connected at the knees. It makes it all quite shocking, really. Because they say that determines it, you know."

"Determines what?" Nate says.

"How happy you'll be in your own marriage. However happy your parents were in theirs, you tend to match it, or something like it. You tend to emulate whatever you saw in your house."

"That's ridiculous," Maggie says.

They both turn to stare at her. She feels her face flush red. She wasn't planning on saying that out loud, wasn't planning on saying anything out loud, but she just wants Murph to go away. Now.

Maggie clears her throat. "I just mean that lots of people can end up in happy marriages, even if they had a rough start of things. Even if they aren't sure they have the best model."

"Your parents suck too, then?" Murph says.

"Excuse me?"

But then instead of answering, she turns to Nate. "So I'll probably be coming by. You know how Louis and Marsha love to party . . . and I can't disappoint the parents."

"Good, we'd like that."

She gives them both a small wave and heads back to the front, as the bus kicks into motion, pulling them down Forty-first Street toward the highway, as the ticket agent comes down the aisle, handing each passenger a small pack of pretzels, a container of water. Collecting fifty-one dollars for their round-trip rides.

Once the agent is gone, Nate leans in close to Maggie, wraps his arm around the back of her shoulders.

"She's okay, Maggie. Once you get to know her a little better. She's not a bad person."

"I believe it. That was nice of her to give you two bags of pretzels. I think most people got one."

"Maggie," Nate says. "I'm talking about Murph."

"I know who you are talking about."

"I'm sorry she made you uncomfortable."

Maggie shakes her head. "She didn't," she says. *You did.* "But what was she talking about with the marriage stuff?"

"What do you mean?"

"Well, when you told her that we were engaged, why was she saying that she was surprised you'd get married? It's not like you're twenty or something. You're thirty-three. Why would that be surprising?"

"I don't remember her saying that," he says. And he gets a look across his face, a look that Maggie doesn't recognize.

"Nate . . ."

"What?"

"You're lying to me now?"

"No, I'm not."

But she knows he is. She knows it, in her gut. And yet she is too tired to guess why. It's still the morning. They still have the entire day ahead of them. She'd rather just believe him.

"You know what?" she says. "Let's just not talk about it right now. Let's listen to some music for a while, okay? I can get some sleep, maybe."

He smiles, relieved, which has the opposite effect on Maggie. "Okay."

He pulls out the iPod. They have a splitter, so they can listen to the same song. And when she guesses which song he is going to pick, that feels like something too. "Moving Pictures, Silent Films," by Great Lake Swimmers. He played it for her, for the first time, a month after they started dating, when they took a weekend road trip to Wyoming. They were driving the back roads into Cody—through all of that gorgeous orange rock, more like outer space than anything she'd ever encountered on this earth—and Nate put on this song. *I think you'll like this,* he said. And she fell in love with it. And with him.

"Pause it for just a sec," she says now. And she squeezes his shoulder, walks over him to the bathroom, to splash some water on her face, hoping to feel better, shake off the malaise settling over her.

But there, as if waiting for her—and not just waiting for the bathroom also—is Murph.

"We meet again."

Maggie tries to smile. "We do."

"Have you used one of these jitney bathrooms before? If not, I should warn you. It's complicated."

"Is it?"

Murph nods. "You need to angle yourself in there just right, or the door slams on your cold, bare ass just as your hand gets stuck in the toilet. Whatever you do, angle left."

"Good tip," Maggie says.

"You will see just how good, especially if you don't follow it. Trust me on that . . ."

Maggie laughs. Maybe Murph isn't the enemy here. Or, really, who cares? Murph, or no Murph. Isn't it beside the point? Maggie is just tired, too tired to be rational. But here is her attempt: she is just going to calm down, to stop thinking about Nate's confession this morning, to stop worrying about the details of his past he left out, to stop letting their immediate future—this divorce party weirdness—stand for more than it is worth.

"Nate is a great guy. You know that, right? Probably better than me. You don't need me to tell you. But everyone's always thought that. He was always the most popular guy in school."

"The most popular out of eleven?"

"Exactly." She pushes her hair out of her face, smiles at Maggie. "Anyway, I'm just really excited for you. It's a nightmare to try to find a good guy. Most guys today, they think if they show up, that's enough. They think if they put a hand on the small of your back, they deserve some sort of award. You know what I mean?"

Maggie smiles. "Kind of," she says.

"We used to always have sex in my parents' bathroom. Nate and I. They have this enormous bathtub with this crazy padding. God, we had no idea what we were doing. Like the first fifty times, we just had *no idea*."

Maggie falls silent.

She almost falls.

"But whatever. Practice makes perfect, right? You can thank me later that he is such a good kisser."

This is when the bathroom door opens, an old guy steps out, zipping his fly, and Murph steps inside, left side first.

Then Murph winks at Maggie, closes the door, and is gone.

Gwyn

It comes from being a minister's daughter, she thinks. She's not good at anger. Not built to hold a grudge. From the time she was old enough to remember, she was taught again and again that anger—or giving in to it, at least—was wrong. Whenever anyone was cruel to her, she was told to forgive. As if it were that easy. In her house, it was supposed to be.

There was that time when Gwyn was eight, and Mia Robinsky from her second-grade class announced that cool girls had curly hair, and the best way to get it was to use peanut butter. She handed Gwyn a jar of peanut butter. And Gwyn used the entire thing, covering her clean blond locks from top to bottom with curlerlike knots of the chunky, sticky mess. Until it hardened. Like Mia directed.

It was her father who washed Gwyn's hair out in the kitchen sink—using a mix of ketchup and vinegar—while Gwyn screamed from the burning and the tearing, more strands coming out than staying in. Even then—in the face of his daughter's hysterics—her father was unflappable.

"Gwyn, love," he said. "Mia is a work in progress. She is just learning how to be."

"How to be? How to be what? A bitch!"

Her father slapped her. Not exactly hard, but there it was. A slap across the bottom of her face, across her jawline. This was one of only two times he was physical with her during her childhood—the other was when she got into her mother's makeup bag and almost cut the tip of her thumb off with a pair of scissors she found in there. He had hit her hand where she cut herself. To warn her away from hurting herself. Being angry at others, apparently, not offering them constant compassion, was equally injurious.

This was a lesson she relearned every time a church congregant would come by the house in pain, or with a grievance. It didn't seem to matter what the specifics were. They blur together now: the man hysterical about his pregnant wife leaving him; the woman whose dying mother refused to talk to her; the husband whose ex-wife lost their life savings in a pyramid scheme. The worst stories anyone could imagine. And always her father's voice rang out with its same, gentle mantra: *We have to figure out how to let go, and forgive. This is our job.*

She wonders if this is why her father never focused too much on the things she did well, the ways she succeeded. Because it might make her feel entitled to be treated a certain way, make her feel like she *should* be angry if someone wasn't honoring her.

Let go. This is the job.

Gwyn circles back around the airport, back past the LOW FLYING PLANES sign, to find Thomas by the curb in a white crewneck sweater and khaki pants, his bags by his feet, his eyes fixed on the digital clock by the airport entrance.

He looks angry. He is angry with her, she imagines, because she wasn't here when he arrived, a little angry that she hasn't been picking up her cell phone, telling him what it is that he is supposed to do. But his face seems to relax as she gets closer, as he realizes she hasn't abandoned him. He breaks into a smile, waves. He is like her father this way, unflappable. Or mostly unflappable. Like her father. Like Buddha.

She can't help but smile back. She loves his face. Even now. People say you get over that with time. If you stay married long enough, you get over someone's face. You stop noticing. But Gwyn never has. Even if they are apart for only a few days, when she sees him again, she is surprised by how his face affects her, makes her think, *Hey, I get this person. Hey, this face is mine.* There are wrinkles now, too, of course, but in Gwyn's opinion they just help carve out the parts of him that looked a little too boyish before. Now he looks confident. Like more good days than bad have brought him here. To his current moment on this earth. It is enough, in its complacency, to make someone cringe—to make Gwyn, in her current moment on this earth, come close.

"There you are," he says. And he puts his bags in the backseat. He doesn't seem to notice the briefcase. He reaches over and touches the tip of her nose with his index finger as he gets into the passenger side. It is the strange and sweet way he often used to greet her. He hasn't done it in a while, which makes Gwyn think it means something. And maybe it does. But probably not what Gwyn wants it to mean.

"I was about to give up on you," he says.

"That makes two of us," she says.

She pulls the car out of the airport, heading away from the potentially crowded main road, opting to wind them around toward the side roads that will lead them back to Montauk, that will lead them the long way home. She stays focused on looking out the windshield, on her hands on the steering wheel, on avoiding Thomas's gaze.

Out of the corner of her eye, she watches as he unbuckles his sandals, putting his left foot up on the dashboard. His bad foot, as he says. The foot missing the third toe, since a surfing accident where it got chopped straight off. Fifteen years ago now. Truth be told, it's one of Gwyn's favorite parts of her husband—that bad foot. When things were better between them, she would stare at it, at the small opening, liking that she was the only one in his adult life to be there on both sides of it. The before and after.

"So," he says. "What's been going on around here?"

She shakes her head. "Not too much, really. I'm having trouble getting in touch with the caterer about tonight, which is making me a little tense. And your daughter—"

He smiles. "*My* daughter today?"

"Your daughter, yes," she says. When Georgia graduated from UCLA's photography program, when she made the masthead at *Rolling Stone* (Asst. Photo Ed.: Georgia G. Huntington), she was Gwyn's daughter. Even when she started dyeing her hair pink earlier this year (wasn't she supposed to be interested in that ten years ago?), but today she belongs to Thomas.

"She's a little prickly because Denis ran into some trouble with a corkscrew. She wants you to call her to talk about it. Or call him in Omaha."

Thomas rolls down the window, and she can see him thinking. "So Denis isn't here yet?" he says. "But I thought he was flying in last night. I thought he promised her that."

This is news to Gwyn, but she has no reason to doubt it. Georgia tends to discuss things with her father that she doesn't tell Gwyn. She may feel judged by Gwyn, or maybe she just knows that even if Thomas is judging her, she won't have to hear about it. That's probably closer to it. Thomas is too nonconfrontational. He never says critical words, especially to their kids. So when she and Thomas had a bad feeling about the decisions Nate was making for himself after high school, or when Georgia dropped out of college for a while, it was up to Gwyn to do something about it. To talk to their children, or not. To be the bad guy, or not. Should she be mad at Thomas about this? She knew it going into their marriage, so it feels beside the point to hold it against him now. She has plenty of other things to hold against him.

"What can I do from here anyway?" Thomas asks.

"Tell him to get on the plane."

He nods, agreeing. And he starts to say something else, but stops himself. They are both avoiding the temptation to address the topic of tonight in too much detail. But she can see—visibly see in his eyes—Thomas remind himself what he does think he should bring up: information about his trip, and, more specifically, what he did during his trip that pertains to Buddhism. As if Gwyn has forgotten that Thomas's newfound spirituality is the reason they are here in the first place, as if she needs proof that it still matters to him.

The part of her that is still her husband's friend wants to remind him that he shouldn't try this hard, that trying this hard is a dead giveaway that you are up to something. But he is already talking, and no one, least of all Gwyn, has the energy to stop him.

"So I had a little time off Thursday, and headed to this incredible temple out in Orange County. It is the second oldest Buddhist temple in the United States."

"No kidding?"

He nods, not sensing her sarcasm—not sensing that she couldn't care less about all of it, everything he is going to say next.

"One of the best parts is that every spiritual director there comes from the same bloodline." He is quiet for a minute, as if thinking about it. "Isn't that amazing? I really was inspired, just being there. It was, far and away, the most beautiful temple I've ever seen."

She nods her head, too, hoping that is enough affirmation so he shuts up.

"I'm thinking about going back out there," he continues.

Apparently not.

"They are sponsoring a silent meditation retreat in November out in the Santa Ynez Valley. Two weeks."

She decides she has done her part, and doesn't say anything else, focuses on the road. The morning is slipping away, the day carving out ahead of them: sunshine and warm air, blue skies as far as the eye can see. This is why she was excited to move out here, originally. Days like this. Drives like this. Instead of spending Saturday afternoons the terrible ways that people in a city can spend Saturdays—shopping, eating too much brunch, seeing friends they half wish they weren't seeing—she and Thomas would be out here together. Taking long car rides, the radio playing some forgotten song, watching the world around them. Gwyn would make sandwiches for lunch. And they would stop in a quiet restaurant for a fried fish dinner or a decent steak, good cheap wine.

She had this pair of cut-off jean shorts she liked to wear for these rides. They were white and tiny, crawling only to the top of her thighs, cutting her in just the right way so that her thighs looked brown and round and endless. Thomas used to hold her there, at the short's edges, most of the day, his hands between her bare thighs.

The last time she put those shorts on must be eight years ago now, those Saturday afternoon rides a thing of the past. Thomas had been traveling to a lot of conferences that fall, and Georgia had just left for her freshman year of college, and Gwyn started spending her newfound free time with Moses Wilder, a dentist in town. (A divorced dentist! Could there be anything less sexy? Maybe only one named Moses.)

Moses Wilder.

It was all innocent enough at first. Moses had two big sheepdogs, and she would go with him when he'd walk them in the morning. She would go for walks with him, and those dogs, and let him pay attention to her. It got less innocent, she guesses, when she began going on the evening walks as well, and let them end with a glass of bourbon on Moses's porch, and a different kind of attention. But one evening, she wore the shorts to meet him. And after he handed her the bourbon and sat down beside her, he reached for her, the same way Thomas used to, and it could have been Thomas's hand on her thighs, it could have been Thomas, and that was too much.

She never saw Moses again. She did what she had to do. She threw herself back into her house, her home, back into Thomas in the ways she still could. She threw out the shorts. She only let herself cry for Moses once. This doesn't make her anyone's hero. This is just what you do. When you put a marriage first. When you remember what you promised. When you want to remember and make it count.

"Have you seen my cell phone, by the way?" Thomas turns toward her, putting his hand on the back of her seat. "I was sure

I packed it, but I got to California and couldn't find it any-where."

Gwyn squeezes the steering wheel. "No, I haven't seen it."

"Are you sure? I don't think I brought it with me."

"Are you expecting me to change my mind if you ask enough times?" she asks, harsher than she means to. She tries to think of a way to dial back, make it less aggressive. But this is how she feels toward Thomas—aggressive. This is what she is learning, how things shift inside when you hide the truth. They shift ir-reconcilably. She takes a deep breath in, forces herself to stay calm. "Maybe it will just show up."

"How do you figure?"

She shrugs. "Lose something else, throw your keys out the window, and look for them instead. And, right then, when you really start looking for your keys, like under the bed, or in the backyard. Bam."

"Bam?"

"There the cell phone will be."

He smiles at her, really smiles at her, because he likes it when he thinks she is being weird, quirky. He finds it endear-ing, and she knows it reminds him of who he thinks she used to be, who he thinks she isn't exactly anymore. When things were easier between them. But before she can enjoy it, the small re-turn of affection, her cell phone starts to ring, PRIVATE coming up on the caller ID.

She motions for him to give her a minute, and picks it up. "This is Gwyn."

"Ms. Lancaster?"

Lancaster. Her maiden name. So she knows immediately who it is. Eve. Eve, the Caterer. Finally. She has her on the phone. This is what she needed to make sure everything is on track for tonight.

Gwyn covers the receiver, sneaks a look at her husband. He is looking out the window, paying no attention to the conversation whatsoever.

"I just got your messages from this morning," Eve says. "I'm sorry about that. I was surfing, and we had no cell phone coverage to speak of, but . . ."

But. Gwyn stops listening, wants to hear the rest of what her husband is saying instead. "You know," she says. "I'm going to have to call you back, okay?"

She flips the phone shut, turns back to her husband.

"Sorry, what were you saying?"

"I don't know," he says. "I was just thinking . . . it must be something about the way we were talking . . . but I was thinking about those Saturday rides we used to take, those long rides. Something about this road, maybe. Something about the way you're taking us home is making me think of it."

She is silent. *Me too,* she could have said. Because she was thinking it too. She got there even before he did. But she doesn't want to give him this. She doesn't want to say anything.

"Do you remember the first time I taught you to drive a stick shift? We went out to McCully's old vineyard. What ever happened to McCully? Do you think he's still around? My God, you were so scared. Why were you so scared? You were such a natural at it. Well, once you could figure out the difference between first and third."

And he laughs. She tries not to. She bites the inside of her lip and tries not to laugh too. This is the painful part. Love doesn't leave you. Not all at once. It creeps back in, making you think it can be another way, that it can still be another way, and you have to remind yourself of the reasons that it probably won't be.

"Thomas," she says. "That was forever ago."

"So you don't remember?"

Third and fifth. The ones that she had trouble with were third and fifth. He had tried to talk to her about making an *H*—but she couldn't seem to do it. And they had to pull over because they were laughing so loud. They couldn't seem to communicate, but that was funny then.

"Gwyn?"

She hates him now. She actually may hate him. "I don't want to," she says.

Maggie

They are the very last stop.

It comes at almost three hours exactly. It comes after too many towns, too many abrupt stops and starts, too many tennis courts and Olympic-size swimming pools and horse farms named things like Happy Meadows or Spring Blossoms. It isn't crowded, this late in September. But still, Maggie has been looking intently out the window and is able to gauge it in quick bursts, the weirdness of the Hamptons, beyond these obvious excesses: the daughter-and-mom duo in their matching yellow Juicy sweatsuits, a caravan of antique convertibles driven by teenage boys, an ice cream parlor for dogs.

But then, after the East Hampton stop, something seems to change—the universe course-correcting itself. Suddenly the roads and towns become more like beach towns that Maggie remembers from growing up: fewer fancy SUVs, more swaying trees and empty spaces.

Clapboard houses that look lived in.

By the time they pull into Montauk's town center, into the bus station, Maggie is looking forward to checking out Nate's hometown, wants to breathe in the sea air, breathe in the beach.

But the windows won't open. It isn't an option. So she closes her eyes and waits.

Nate leans in and kisses her cheek, then kisses her right below the jaw. "We're here," he says.

"That's something," she says.

He smiles. "That is something."

She takes his hand, squeezes. She is trying. She is really trying to let the day start again, right here, when she needs it the most.

And by the time they step off the bus, Murph is already out of sight. Maggie decides to take this as the first good sign. The second one is that, as soon as Maggie is on solid ground and gets a look around, she feels intrigued by the town around her.

Montauk isn't what she expected—it feels less like she's walked into a beach town and more like she's walked into a ghost town: an empty police station and a closed-down restaurant, a sign for the Memory Motel out ahead of them, and in the distance, just a peek of ocean.

"You ready for this?" Nate says, as she looks around. "Because, if not, this thing turns itself around in about twenty minutes. We'll head back to New York City. Be home in time to watch the sun go down."

"Be home in time to watch *Weeds*?" she says.

"Even be home in time to buy a television to watch it on," he says. "Just tell me when you're ready to get out of here."

She steps on his tiptoes, and whispers softly into his ear. "I'm ready to get out of here."

And he reaches for her, because he thinks she is flirting a little. And part of her is—the part of her that is trying to overpower the other part, the part that wants to scream: *I am ready now! Because it is all starting to feel manageable again between*

us, to feel something like normal, and just when that happens to-
day, I seem to get struck down worse. I hear about you having sex
in mansion/high schools with padded bathtubs.

But she takes a deep breath, and follows him across the
street to the small parking lot next to John's Pancake House,
where they are supposed to meet his sister. There is a small
taffy stand outside the restaurant, a group of teenagers in
matching green Windbreakers with s.h.s. weather club written on the back, standing around sipping sodas and eating
taffy. Maybe they are on a class trip. Maggie doesn't know, but
she feels a longing to be among them, to have access to the day
ahead of them: sticky candy, and conversations about water
currents, and a bus ride back to wherever they're coming
from.

Only before she can think too much about it, one of the girls,
who Maggie assumes is with them, steps out from behind the
hood of a dirty gray Volvo wagon, revealing the pregnant bulge
in her belly.

Her stomach is a dead giveaway, even if she weren't identical
to the most recent photo on their refrigerator: same pink streaks
running through her blond hair, wearing an X-large nofx tank
top and faded jeans, wearing Nate's eyes.

Georgia. In the photograph, she was cradling her stomach.
Now, she is cradling a three-pound plastic sand bucket of salt-
water taffy in both of her hands. And when she looks up, she is
sucking on one of the pinkish-green strands, like it is a cigarette, like it is the last cigarette on earth.

"Nathaniel," she says. "You're here."

"I'm here," he says.

Which is when she turns to Maggie.

"And you're here!"

Maggie waves hip-side—small, shy—and Nate drops his bag, letting go of her hand and moving toward his sister.

He bends down to give her a hug, an overly gentle hug, as though he'll break her. Maggie laughs, knowing this is what he is worried about, and because it is so nice to watch him with Georgia. Even with her huge stomach, even holding on to that huge taffy tub, she looks so small next to Nate. She looks like she belongs to him.

When Georgia pulls away, she holds out her hand for Maggie, who takes it.

"I'm glad to meet you," Maggie says.

"I'm glad to meet you too," she says. "You don't smoke by chance, do you?"

"No, she doesn't, Georgia," Nate says.

"Was I talking to you? I was asking *Maggie*."

"And I am telling you that Maggie doesn't."

Georgia turns back to Maggie. "No one is asking anyone to give me one. But someone's going to have to smoke a cigarette for me. Sometime soon. And I thought maybe you looked up to the task?"

Maggie smiles at her. "I'm not sure if that is a compliment, but I can do that."

"Excellent."

"Can you not attempt to kill my girlfriend as soon as you meet her?" Nate says.

Georgia rolls her eyes, and she rolls them again in case he missed it. Then she hands Nate the keys, and opens the back-seat door for herself. "You can drive. I'm lying down in the back with my tub o' candy." She pauses, points her finger at him. "But

I feel the need to warn you that if you tell me I'm huge, or that I'm growing, or that I look anything but like the most gorgeous pregnant person you've ever seen, I'm going to toss this candy at you. Even if it runs us off the road."

Nate opens the passenger side door for Maggie, winking at her. "So maybe this isn't the best time to say that you look like a house?"

Georgia slams Nate in the arm with the taffy, and Maggie starts to laugh. "Any brothers?" Georgia asks.

Maggie shakes her head. "I wish."

Georgia pulls on her taffy, throws a piece at her brother, hitting him on the arm. "Really? Even now?"

"Less so," she says, and they all get in the car—Nate and Maggie up front. But instead of lying down like she said she was going to, Georgia wraps her hand around the back of the driver's seat, and sticks her head between the two front seats.

"So we need to talk, Nate," she says.

"You don't waste any time," he says.

He is just pulling out of the parking space, and down the main street of town: restaurants and surfing stores appearing on Maggie's left, the beach and ocean getting larger on her right until she can hear the water, feel its breeze.

"Well, if you ever called back your *pregnant* sister, I wouldn't be so anxious. But you need to be prepared. You need to be prepared before we get back to the house. It's like the twilight zone around here."

Maggie immediately feels uncomfortable, like she shouldn't be present for this. So she rolls down the window, tries to listen to whatever is happening outside.

But Georgia taps her on the shoulder. "Can you close that? I need you to hear me. Because I'm going to need you for backup."

"For what?" Maggie asks.

"For when Nate pretends this isn't a big deal, and you're going to have to help me convince him that it is."

Nate looks at her in the rearview mirror. "What are you talking about?"

"Well, for one thing, Dad is like a huge Buddhist."

"A huge Buddhist?" Nate laughs. "I don't think you can be a huge Buddhist."

"It has become his *whole* life, Nate. There is nothing else he wants to talk about. Like when I miss Denis or something, he keeps telling me to live in the present moment. To let myself be present. It's all I can do to not say, '*Presently* you are being a total ass.'"

"Georgia . . ." Nate says.

"Mom is not acting like herself either," she continues. "They say this divorce is amicable, but they both seem like they swallowed a box of pills to get there."

Nate is quiet, as they drive out of town and up into the hills. He points to a structure no bigger than a dot, far out in the distance. "We used to jump off that bridge when we were kids. You can't see it clearly from here, but there's this great roof on the top—"

"Nate! Come on, man!" Georgia says. "You're not even listening to me. Please listen to me."

"I'm listening," he says. "But this is what Dad *and* Mom want, remember? Don't you want that for them? We're not kids anymore. And they're definitely not. Maybe you should be focusing on your own . . . situation."

"What's that supposed to mean? Because I'm not married, Denis and I could fall apart at any minute?" She drills Nate with a dirty look, as if he is missing everything, and turns to Maggie.

"You understand what I'm saying, right, Maggie? You understand this isn't good?"

"Which part?" Maggie asks.

"How fucked up things are about to get," she says.

Maggie watches Nate turn on the blinker, fights her urge to ask him why he is not chiming in—why he seems to have no opinion about any of this? Why he seems not only calm, but, also, unbelievably . . . removed.

But before she can say a thing, Nate takes another right into an area called Ditch Plains: small cabana houses, a low-rise condominium, the beach and ocean out before them. And then they are heading toward it, heading to a street marked PRIVATE, a threat of prosecution if they drive through. Nate does anyway, driving all the way down the road—past several long driveways and high gates—until he has arrived at the farthest one, a small rock in front of the drive with white paint on it, reading: HUNTINGTON HALL.

Why does that sound familiar to Maggie? Maggie doesn't know, not until they drive farther down the driveway and his family's house comes into view. And then it hits her, in a bright flash, almost like a home movie: zoom in on a large oversize cardboard box of postcards. Pan out to a childhood bedroom, Maggie's bedroom, Maggie sitting in the corner, poring over the postcards. She would do this for hours. In fact, that was what she wanted to do when she was a kid. She wanted to make postcards. She figured to make them, you had to be able to go to all the places where the pictures were taken.

She loves those postcards. They are the one possession she has held on to, still safe in her childhood room. These hundreds of postcards, many of them she still knows by heart. This is why the name resonated with her. Huntington Hall, Hunt Hall. On the back of the postcard, that was how it was labeled: *Hunt Hall, Summer Cottage.* A photograph of the house, life-size before her now: this Victorian home with beautiful white pillars, an enormous wraparound porch, a windmill on top of the third story, cliffside surrounding it, as far as the eye sees.

"There is a postcard of your house?" she says. She turns toward Nate. "You grew up in a postcard?"

"You have a copy of it?" Georgia says. "How cool!"

Which is when Georgia's phone starts to ring.

"It's Denis!" Georgia says. "Stop the car."

And just as Nate does, she reaches over the front seat, takes the keys from the ignition and is out of the car, leaving the door open, and racing away from them, racing toward somewhere she can speak to Denis in private. Maggie watches her stop by the steps leading to the porch, flipping her phone open, her free hand instinctively wrapping around her stomach.

She keeps her eyes on Georgia, focuses on her and not on the house behind her, or on Nate, until he slides over into the passenger seat, moving her onto his lap, his hand cupping her leg. She doesn't know exactly why it comes to her, but it does: a memory of the two of them sitting, similar to this, in a hospital emergency room, near her father's house, after she dropped a speaker on her foot. She had been carrying it across the bar, the first time Nate came home with her, and she dropped it, slicing her ankle open. Nate sat with her all night in that hospital room, holding ice there, waiting as she moved to the front of the triage line for a doctor to sew her ankle up, tell her she could go home.

Maybe the memory comes back so strongly because the only other time she was in that hospital, she had been there alone, after breaking her wrist during a lacrosse game in high school. She hadn't even been able to reach her father, let alone count on his caretaking abilities.

"I can't believe you grew up here . . ." she says, and shakes her head.

"Are you overwhelmed?"

"Why would I be?" she says. "I don't even have to worry about meeting your parents. I can pitch a tent on the cliff, and hide from them all weekend if I want."

"Very funny," he says. He smiles at her, happy. "But you like it?"

"Who wouldn't like it?" She points at an acre of clearing near a swing, or what looks like a swing, near the edge of the cliff. "We could build a yurt for ourselves right there."

"Well, that would involve coming back with some frequency."

"And why is that a bad thing?"

He squeezes her knee, and, for a moment, he looks like he remembers something all over again, something he has to tell her. She doesn't understand why: he has told her already, right? The financial stuff is already out there, the Champ name thing, even the high school nightmare-of-a-girlfriend thing. What else could he be worried about?

Before she can ask, she hears a screech of tires and turns to look out of the back windshield, just in time to see a large white van with two surfboards on the roof come barreling into the driveway, backward. The van is within an inch of them, of their car, before the driver slams on the brakes, but not quickly enough, the van lurching backward again, in two final jolts, and hitting the back of their wagon—hard.

Maggie jerks forward, her hand reaching for the dashboard,

her head banging against her forearm, Nate bumping into her shoulder. Double impact.

"Jesus . . ." Nate says. "Are you okay?"

She feels around herself, feels her head. Nothing hurts, exactly, or not a lot. But it startles her, makes her lose her bearings for a second. She shakes out her head, opens and closes her eyes hard, tries to get them back. She saw the whole thing happen but couldn't stop it, now she is seeing it again.

"I'm fine," she says. "Are you fine?"

He nods. They get out of the car and head to the back to survey the damage, to see who it was that hit them. The other driver is flipping the van around so the front is facing them, and then she is out of her vehicle too. It is a woman, around their age—with red hair in low-flying braids, and a too-large chef's jacket. She is staring at their bumper, and holding her hands to her head, her fingers running through the braids.

"Holy shit!" she says. "Holy. Holy. Holy. Holy. HOLY."

Maggie follows the woman's eye down to the indent she has made, the deep crack by the taillight. If it were a new car, as opposed to this old wagon, maybe the damage would look worse. But in the context of the rips and tears on the bumper alone, it is not that big of a deal. It isn't a big deal unless you know to look for it, to make it one.

"I can't believe I did that," she says. "I was just trying to back in so I could turn around . . ." She points back toward the edge of the driveway, toward the direction she came from. "And I guess I wasn't paying good attention, or I was paying attention to the wrong thing, because I flipped in here and I saw you in the rearview and I tried to stop but I should have just tapped the brake and I hit it too hard, and she bounced backward like she does and you know the rest . . ."

Maggie is staring at her face. Up close, she looks older than Maggie would have thought from a distance. Maggie is guessing she isn't—is guessing that her first instinct is right and she is in her late twenties, probably younger than Maggie. Her body still young and wily, but her face weathered, creased, from too many days at the beach, in the ocean. Her face holding on to a little too much sadness.

"I'm so sorry," she says. "I didn't wreck your car, did I? It doesn't look like I did much of anything, but it's hard to know. We should probably bring it in somewhere."

Nate shrugs his shoulders. "Don't worry about it. It's a very old car. It's seen worse hits than that. Probably today alone."

"Really?" The woman looks totally relieved, motions behind herself. "Because I am catering this party next door tonight, and it's a big deal. I've spent the last thirty-six hours getting ready."

Maggie looks at the surfboards on top of the roof that are slightly wet and glossy, just used. Then she looks into the van, notices a guy sleeping in the passenger side.

"Or most of the last thirty-six hours," she adds.

Maggie blushes, feeling caught. "I didn't mean anything by that."

"No, no . . . I mean, between us, I shouldn't be catering this big of a party, but I didn't know how to say no. Doing this gig tonight will pay my rent for a year. It will pay it for two years. Who could say no to that?"

Maggie shrugs. "No one."

"But anyway, the housekeeper next door—at the Buckleys'?— is all confused, and told me to come over here. She says the party I'm catering is over here. That seems unlikely. I may be out of it, but I'm not that out of it."

Maggie looks over at Nate, trying to ask him with her eyes: *The Buckleys as in Murphy Buckley?*

But he doesn't respond, reaching out to shake the caterer's hand. "You're Eve?"

"How did you know?"

He points to the big *Eve's Kitchen,* which is written in blue cursive lettering on the right side of the van. It has painted tomatoes all over it—in yellows, greens, and reds. Vines running between them, all along the front, down to the windshield.

Her face relaxes. "Yes, I'm Eve. And over here in the passenger seat is Tyler." She bangs on the window, and Tyler wakes up, albeit briefly, and gives them the peace sign.

Maggie gives him one back.

"I'm Nate. And this is Maggie. And that over there . . ." He points at Georgia, who is picking at a bush, still talking to Denis. "That is my sister. Apparently, she can't be disturbed while on the phone, even for a car accident."

Eve nods. "Got it. Do not disturb pregnant sister when she is on the phone."

Nate smiles. "So, I'm a little behind. Are the Buckleys having a party too, or aren't they?"

"No, the Lancasters."

"The Lancasters?" He gives her a confused look. "Gwyn Lancaster, you mean? That's my mother. That's her maiden name. This is the right house, right here." He points at Hunt Hall.

Eve pulls a small red notebook out of her pocket—a drawing of Karl Marx on the front. She looks between it and the house, like either might give her a clue about what she is missing.

"Weird," she says. "I have written down that I am supposed to go next door."

"Maybe she just wanted you to set up over there. The Buckleys are good friends of ours, so it's possible."

Good friends of ours? Maggie gives Nate a look, which he either misses or ignores. *They are?*

Nate is still looking at Eve. "Has my mother been difficult? My sister seems to think this party is causing her strain."

"Your mother? Oh, no, she's been lovely. I think her previous caterer had to cancel last minute. She just called me two days ago about this, totally desperate." She pauses. "But nice, even in the desperation. And offering me a lot of money. Too much money. But I guess if you're having two hundred people at your house—"

"Two hundred?" Maggie says, turning to Nate. *I thought tonight was small. . . .*

Nate shrugs back, and for a second she thinks it is to say, *Me too.* But she sees the recognition fall over his face, as though he has been told tonight is this big, and has just forgotten to tell Maggie, or even to acknowledge it to himself.

"Well, let me get the keys from my sister so we can get out of your way, so you can get inside, and started." He calls out to Georgia, but she doesn't answer him, not even to say one second. So Nate gets louder, starts walking toward her. "Hey, Miss Huntington! Can we borrow those keys for a second?"

Eve reaches out and touches Maggie's arm. "Wait, what did he just call his sister?"

Maggie turns and looks at Eve, who is looking more than a little pale and uncomfortable. She is confused at first, trying to put the chain of conversation back in order.

"You mean when he called her Miss Huntington? That's her name, Georgia Huntington."

"And he's Nate Huntington? And so . . . they are the chil-dren of Gwyn and Thomas? Their parents are Thomas and Gwyn Huntington."

The last part doesn't seem like a question, so Maggie doesn't answer, just stands there watching Eve compose herself, and wondering if they are *that* well known, her future in-laws, that intimidating. That a socialist surfer-chick—who strikes Maggie as someone who rarely allows herself to get too worked up about anything—looks like she'd rather do anything than deal with them?

Maggie's eyes inadvertently sweep back to the house. The widow's walk near the top, luminous in the air. And she can guess at it: Gwyn using her maiden name to avoid this very mo-ment when Eve is freaked out. Why shouldn't she be? She imag-ines a party like this could be potentially huge for a young caterer. Lots of people with lots of money, who want to utilize the hot, new thing for their next event. For their next Friday night dinner, for their next clambake.

Eve looks beyond freaked out by this proposition, which makes Maggie feel compelled to joke, balance things out. "See, now you're freaking me out here a little," Maggie says. "It's my first time meeting them."

Eve shakes her head, and, as if remembering herself, clears her throat. "Don't be freaked out, I'm sorry," she says. "They are nice people. *I've heard* they're nice people, at least. Mrs. Hun-tington just has a reputation around here."

"A reputation for what?"

"For being Mrs. Huntington."

But just then, before Eve explains, Nate heads back to the car—Georgia's keys in his hand.

"Let me get this car moved for you," he says, walking toward them. "And I'd be happy to help you carry some of this stuff inside. You can't manage all by yourself."

Maggie looks in the back of the van to make out platter after platter of hors d'oeuvres, which, from beneath their plastic covers, seem to be different variations of oversized mushroom caps.

"I'm okay. Tyler and I have it under control. Right, T?" She bangs on the passenger side of the van. The guy inside jerks awake, looks around, and this time stays awake.

"Well, consider this our open invitation to help you today in any way you need," Nate says. "We can do runs for you, locate a hard-to-find vegetable. Even if it means we have to drive an hour away. Two hours away is fine too."

Maggie gives Nate a look as if to say, *very funny*.

Eve smiles. "I'll keep it in mind," she says. "Thank you for the offer."

Maggie reaches out, covers the scratch on the Volvo. "And we'll take care of the damage," she says. "If it even needs to be taken care of. Nate's parents won't have to know."

Maybe it isn't her place to say this, but she decides she'll pay for the scratch if she has to—anything so Eve stops looking like she is about to have a nervous breakdown right in front of them.

"You sure about that?" Eve says.

"Positive," Nate says. "It could have been a lot worse. You have no idea what's waiting for us inside."

Eve laughs at this, a little too loud, like she knows something they don't. Or something they are about to find out. "Well," Eve says. "I guess I'll be seeing you both a little later today."

"Sounds good."

Maggie gets back into the car as Nate drives them to the side of the driveway, out of the way.

Eve gives them a wave and heads back to her truck too. But instead of moving forward toward the house, she puts the truck in reverse and drives straight out of Ditch Plains. As fast as the vine van will carry her.

Nate looks at the now empty driveway, as though he can't believe it. "She's not coming in? What about the mushroom caps?"

"I guess they are going to have to wait."

He shrugs. "Maybe she's just not ready."

Maggie turns back toward the house-slash-national-park in front of her—its pillars like signposts to a world she doesn't exactly want to visit. The large wraparound porch like a promise of something, but maybe nothing she is quite ready to know about yet.

"I know the feeling," she says, as they walk inside.

Gwyn

This is what she remembers.

That first time she came to Montauk with Thomas, to see where he lived, it was winter and freezing out. And she came down here to the edge of the property—to this deep cliff, overlooking the beach below, and stood there, by herself, watching as the sun slowly went down. She was barely twenty-two years old, she was shivering, but standing there on the cliff she saw her life spread out before her. Or maybe that's too easy. Maybe what's closer to the truth is that for the first time she saw something promising in her life, something she didn't want to look away from. Even now, all these years later, she remembers how she felt looking out at that water. She remembers that this was when this place first became hers.

Now, she sits down on the swing—the small, wooden swing—that Thomas's parents gave them as a wedding present. That Champ actually made for them. It is a beautiful swing, and she comes out here daily to sit on it. To read or knit, just have her morning coffee, and look at the paper. Or, like today, to get herself ready for something she doesn't want to do.

That first weekend, though, there was no swing, and she stood there getting ready for all she did want to do.

Thomas had been so nervous to show her where he grew up. He had already started to work at the free clinic out here, so he wasn't only showing her his past; he was showing her their future. If she decided to join him in it. They would live here, at the end of the world, which at the time—in theory—felt romantic. But seeing it firsthand in the middle of a cold, cold winter felt like something more complex, closer to something he had explained: *You'll either love the quiet or you won't be able to take it. And that will make all the difference. It will make all the difference in whether you can imagine this becoming your life, too.*

It was then she started to understand that it wouldn't just be her and Thomas out here, but this third component—the house itself—that would dictate things for them. This house, in its isolation, which would demand that their marriage be both stronger and looser than if they lived somewhere else. Somewhere urban or suburban—somewhere less close to the edge of the earth, that required less partnership to make things work. That, quite simply, required less.

Thomas doesn't know this part. She went into town that first afternoon to get some fresh juice, and called her sister from a pay phone on the side of Old Montauk Highway, wondering why it was that it took her until now to understand that she was being asked to step into someone else's already-chosen life. Or step out.

"What do you want from me?" Jillian asked her.

"I want you to tell me that you like him," she said. "I want you to tell me it will turn out okay."

"I like him, Gwyn," she said. "And it is probably not going to turn out okay."

"How can you know that?"

"Because you only ever ask me questions when you need to hear an answer you can't tell yourself."

Then Jillian stopped giving any opinion. She reminded her instead of something her father did when they moved into that colonial house in Macon—Gwyn barely four years old—the house her parents would stay in until they died. He told the girls that when they grew up and found the place they wanted to make their home, they should find a safe spot there and make three wishes. They could count on three coming true, but only three, so they should wish carefully.

It probably stuck with Jillian, and should have stuck with Gwyn, because their father never said things like this. Superstitious things. But he believed you got to make three wishes for being brave enough to even imagine a place could become your home.

So that first night—once Gwyn decided she would make Montauk hers—she stood on the edge of this very cliff and did it. She made her wishes. She sealed her fate.

She's never told anyone what she wished for, not even Jillian. And she's never told anyone that she saved the third. She's saved it for the day she needed to wish to overcome something bigger than she could imagine, or plan for: that one of her kids would get better, that the car accident wasn't insurmountable, that death wouldn't get to Thomas before her.

But she's using it now—by the edge of the cliff, her cliff, looking down over it while it still is.

This moment, this wish.

Thomas was completely wrapped up in the first two: her wish that they would marry. Her wish that they would have healthy, happy kids. Such average wishes, so unspecific. He may as well get this one as well.

She gets up off the swing, stands tall. She breathes in the sky, the blue of it, the air collapsing and growing thinner around her. She doesn't feel it yet—or can't name it—the storm that is brewing, but she feels something.

She wishes he will be sorry.

Then she unclasps her hand to find Thomas's cell phone in there. It is small and black. Its red light is flashing brightly. There are messages waiting for him. Phone numbers he may think he needs, but will not have for now.

It is eighty feet to the ocean. She pulls back, takes aim and lets the cell phone fly.

Maggie

There is a statue of Buddha in the living room.

Gold-plated and several feet high, sitting tall against the wall, between the two windows. Smiling.

Maggie is squatting down before him, looking him right in the eye. Looking him right in his smile, his wide cheeks. She wants to reach out and touch him, the Buddha, right where they meet: that smile, those cheeks.

Thomas comes up behind her and hands her a glass of iced tea. "It's over a hundred years old," he says. "I just had it shipped here."

"The Buddha," she says. "Or the tea?"

Thomas laughs, which is good, because as soon as the words are out of her mouth she knows they could have been taken badly. His graciousness seems to confirm Maggie's guess that he is like Nate in that important way: open, nonjudgmental. She still only reluctantly heads back to the couch and sits down across from him. She doesn't want to look at him, not straight on. He looks so much like Nate in person—same nose and hair and eyes. Watching him, Maggie feels a little like she is peering into her own future. This will be Nate in thirty years. This will be what Nate looks like when their son comes home with his fiancée for the first time.

Maggie looks around the rest of the room instead. It is Asian inspired, with warm yellow walls and eight-foot windows, the large beautiful mahogany bookshelves taking up one wall, a painting of a Chinese character taking up the other. Its steady line on the bottom makes it look like a ship. If she thinks about it, this room—what is in it—is probably worth more than her father's entire house. She tries to think about something else.

The Buddha seems to still be laughing at her. She covers the side of her eyes, bites her lip, and tries to listen as Nate's dad starts to tell them about the medical conference, about the temple he visited in Orange County while he was out there.

They are all sitting down now: Nate and her on the couch, Thomas in the big armchair across from them, and Georgia lying on the floor, on her back, beneath him. Gwyn hasn't materialized yet.

"I'm thinking of going back out there for a while and taking some classes," he says. "After things are settled."

"You mean after the divorce is settled?" Georgia says. "You can say it, Dad. We're celebrating it tonight, aren't we?"

"We're celebrating everything that came before it, George," Thomas says.

"How is that different?" she says.

"Because," he says. "It's our way of reminding you that no one is to blame."

Is that an answer? Maggie looks over at Nate, who is nodding his head, like he understands what his dad is saying, and maybe he does—maybe he understands something she doesn't, like how that is an answer to the question Georgia asked. It sounds more, to Maggie, just like an answer Thomas wants to give—regardless of what is being asked of him. So he gets to believe it.

But then, before she can think of why that is striking her, Maggie hears footsteps padding down the hallway, and Gwyn comes flying into the room. Gwyn with her long blond hair, a pale sheath dress running down to her bare feet. She looks like a commercial for herself, and Maggie is forced to see that she will *not* be her when their son comes home with his fiancée: a beautiful woman—her beauty still sharp, graceful and elegant, a close semblance to who she has always been. There are women like this, and Maggie guesses that if you pay attention, you know early on whether you get to be one of them. Probably—if you aren't paying attention—you don't.

Gwyn makes a beeline for Nate and her, bending to give him a large hug, bending before he can even stand.

"It's looking like we're probably going to get a little wet during this party of ours," Gwyn says. "I think a storm is moving in off the horizon. Maybe we should move the whole thing inside . . . what do you think? I don't *want* to move the thing inside, but that barn is falling apart. . . ."

This before hello.

This before anything else.

"Hey there, Champ," she says, as she pulls away. And for a second Maggie's eyes open wide, because she thinks Gwyn is calling him by his *real* name, his birth name, but then she realizes Gwyn is just saying it like a nickname. Like calling him a winner. Like how Maggie sometimes calls him "Sport."

She holds her hand against his cheek. "It's good to see your face," she says. And then, still on her knees, Gwyn turns to Maggie. "And you must be Celine?"

Everyone is silent.

"I'm kidding!" Gwyn squeezes her knee, and then leans forward to hug her, to really hug her. "It is lovely to meet you, Maggie," she says, right into her ear, so only Maggie hears her.

"You too," Maggie says, and smiles.

Maggie makes decisions about people too quickly—she knows this—but she likes Gwyn, right away, partially because she sees what she might have missed if Gwyn hadn't bent to greet her: a sweetness in her eyes. A real sweetness. For a second, it makes her think of all that Nate had growing up. These two loving parents, this home. Even if his parents are splitting up now, it doesn't explain why in the last year and a half he has always seemed less than eager to come back here, and to them.

She tries to shake off her questioning as Gwyn gets up and goes to sit down on the floor beside Georgia, taking Thomas's glass from him and taking a sip, one swift motion, as she plops down on the floor, her dress wrapping her legs—scooting in as close as she can get to her daughter.

"So what did I miss?" Gwyn says. "Did you have an easy trip out here?"

"Fairly easy," Nate says. "Until we got to the driveway."

"What happened in the driveway?"

"Nothing," Nate says, and shakes his head, as if remembering they weren't going to bring it up. "My sister just got out of the car, while I was still driving, to answer a phone call."

"You're telling on me?" Georgia says. "What are you, nine?"

Nate smiles, proud of himself. "I just turned ten," he says.

But then Thomas interrupts them. "You weren't using my

phone, by chance, were you, Georgia? For the phone call? I can't find it."

"Why would I be using your phone?"

"You wouldn't," Gwyn says, putting her hand on Georgia's shoulder, rubbing it. Then she turns to look up at Nate's dad. "Let it go, Thomas. It's gone."

And Maggie is startled by it—startled by it on the heels of thinking that they are so lovely, even in the midst of all of this— what she hears in Gwyn's voice: anger. Latent, maybe, but there nevertheless.

But she looks over at Nate, who seems not to have noticed, and so Maggie decides she has imagined it.

"Hey, the caterer was here, by the way," Georgia says, pointing toward the front of the house, toward the driveway. "And she told Nate and Maggie that there are two hundred people coming tonight. That's a mistake, right?"

"You guys met the caterer?" Gwyn asks, taking her hand off Georgia's shoulder. "Thomas, did you meet the caterer too?"

"Mom, that's kind of beside the point, wouldn't you say? Why are there two hundred people coming to the house? There are supposed to be, like . . . seven," Georgia says.

"We never said seven," Gwyn says.

"You said, *small parting ceremony.*"

"And that equals the number seven?" Gwyn says. "Since when?"

Georgia gives her a look. "Why didn't you give us any warning about this? Because you thought Nate wouldn't come?"

"We did tell Nate," Thomas says.

They did? Maggie looks at Nate. *You knew?*

But Nate doesn't meet her eyes. He is looking down at his

own hands, as if this were a stranger's too-loud conversation in a dentist's office, as if he just wants it to be over. He looks up at his sister. "We've been so crazed with the move and the restaurant," he says. "I guess I wasn't taking it in."

"That's shocking. I've never known *you* to avoid addressing things that you don't want to deal with," Georgia says.

Maggie almost asks aloud, what does that mean? But Georgia is turning back to her mom. "Why didn't you tell me the scale of tonight?"

"We didn't want to overwhelm you while you were pregnant," Thomas says.

"I'm still pregnant."

"Well, we didn't want to overwhelm you while you were less pregnant," Gwyn says. "But there's no need to be upset anyway. Tonight is going to be really lovely. Just a little more *involved* than you thought."

"Define 'involved,'" Georgia says, an edge to her voice.

"Too much food, a large band, and my very delicious red velvet cake. It's kind of like an anniversary party. A big anniversary party. But instead of just celebrating our anniversary . . . we are also celebrating that it is the last one."

"Fantastic," Georgia says.

"Look, what your mom is trying to say is that no one is the villain here," Thomas says. "We still plan on being close. Celebrating your wedding, Georgia's birth. We just want to do those important things in an honest way."

"Who are you talking to, Dad?" Georgia says. "Us or yourself? You just said that five minutes ago."

Gwyn stands up and starts to leave the room. "Well, then let's avoid any of us getting too repetitious and take a breather, okay? Just give ourselves a chance to get used to this. It's not like we are surprising you that we are getting divorced. The rest is just . . . details. In a little bit, it won't feel so severe. In a few hours, even. We'll have some drinks, some good food. Celebrate our family."

Georgia says, "At the divorce party?"

"Yes, at the divorce party."

"I was kidding."

But Gwyn gives her daughter's shoulder a slight squeeze, as if that settles it, and starts to walk out of the room. Only Thomas tries to stop her. "Maybe you should sit until everything is covered," he says.

"Everything, Thomas?"

This is when Maggie notices it, reminiscent of the anger she detected before: Gwyn gives Thomas a look, so quick and brutal that anyone could miss it. And everyone seems to, except for Maggie, who feels like she now knows that something is going on. Something beyond whatever it is Thomas and Gwyn are trying to pretend isn't. But what? Everyone knows they are separating. Amicably separating, but separating nevertheless. What could be worse than that? Perhaps something a little less amicable.

Gwyn is standing in the doorway now, smiling too eagerly. "Tonight is what it is," Gwyn says. "And this time tomorrow, it will be done. If you don't want to come, don't come."

"I don't want to come," Georgia says.

"You're coming," Gwyn says.

And with that, she is gone. Maggie watches her go, the same way she came, in a swirl of white fabric and hair and wind. She looks over at Nate, who is looking back at her.

Are you okay? he asks with his eyes.

If you are, she answers.

"Guys, I get that this isn't exactly easy," Thomas says. "But it is all going to shake out to be for the best, I promise you. In a year, we'll both be better off being apart. We'll have moved on. We'll be able to be true friends, which is something we haven't been able to be in a long time."

"Because of the Buddhism thing?" Georgia says.

"Because of a lot of things," Thomas says.

Maggie looks up at her future father-in-law. There is something different in Thomas's tone—something that sounds like the truth.

"I'm going to be away a lot on retreats and at conferences," Thomas says. "It's better. It's better that your mother isn't always sitting around waiting here for when I come home, for when I am leaving again."

"So don't leave again," Georgia says.

He wraps his arms around his daughter. "Your mom and I are both okay with what is happening. This is what we want for ourselves. Isn't that the most important part?"

"No." But she sighs as she says it—and offers a half smile— as if she has given up the fight. For now. Thomas looks at her gratefully—for this allowance—and turns toward Nate.

"You okay, guy?" Thomas asks him.

"No, he's not okay," Georgia says. "He just doesn't know himself well enough to know he's not okay."

Nate smiles at his sister. "I'm fine, Dad. I just think Maggie and I should unpack," he says.

Maggie looks at Nate. *Where have you been?*

"So unpack," Thomas says. "I'm not going anywhere."

Maggie looks at him, and fights the urge to say it. *If I'm starting to understand anything, it is that that may not be true.* Then, as she stands up, she looks back at the Buddha one last time— wondering what he would say if he could talk. Maybe, Welcome to the family.

More likely, Get ready.

Gwyn

In Buddhism, there is a word that means loving-kindness. *Maitri*. It means always acting from a place where you try to be kind toward yourself, toward others. To meet whatever hand you are dealt, with an open curiosity, and not make it mean everything, not make anything mean more than it should.

Maitri—forgiveness.

What is the expression in Buddhism for 'betrayal'?

How about for fucking liar?

Gwyn stares at herself in the bathroom mirror, her heart pounding out of her chest, beating through her ears. She takes another drag of her joint, breathing deep, trying to calm herself, trying to get centered.

It's done. The hardest part is done. Protecting them, protecting her children. And she thinks she has, thinks they bought the gentler version of the story. She thinks they bought the whole thing. Why wouldn't they? Why wouldn't they assume that what was going on is what she told them is going on?

She assumed it. For a long time. Here, in this very bathroom, she bought it, herself: Gwyn standing by the sink, Thomas sitting on the edge of the bathtub, as he first told her how serious he was getting about Buddhism. His hands clasped around the pamphlet, like a paper witness. He was meeting her eyes in the mirror—they were meeting each other's eyes there. Even then, she knew that was a first step toward not meeting them in real life.

"I'm losing him," she told Jillian over the phone later that week. Her sister lived in Oregon with an underemployed journalist who grew pot in their backyard. And even on beautiful Sundays, the journalist slept until 2 P.M. and wanted to spend the rest of the day in bed. And to think! To think there was a time when Gwyn had felt bad for her.

"You are not losing him," Jillian said. "It's a phase."

"A phase? I don't think so. Deciding to go on safari in Africa is a phase. Or joining a book club! This is a religion. One that he says may take him away to retreats for weeks at a time. Months at a time."

"You have had tough stretches before," Jillian said.

And this was true. They had. Who hadn't? When the kids were little and Thomas hadn't known his place, exactly; when Thomas had taken that yearlong fellowship in Nevada and Gwyn had felt neglected. But still. This time felt different, right from the beginning. For the first time, it felt like they weren't in it together. For the first time, it felt like Thomas was determined to make her feel like they weren't in it together.

Gwyn takes another drag of the joint, feeling the world start to grow foggy, dulled out, in a good way. She never smoked before now, not in high school, only once in college. But when this whole Buddhism thing started, her sister Jillian sent her a small stash of marijuana in the mail, hidden in small sewing thimbles, buried under a plate of brownies. *In case this phase doesn't end by his birthday,* she wrote in the note. *In case, by his birthday, you need to be celebrating something else.*

This had been Jillian's promise. That it would end by his birthday. His sixty-third. Based on Jillian's theory that Thomas was behaving the way a man sometimes does at sixty-three. (*People say it happens at sixty-five, but it is sixty-three,* she said. *That is the birthday when they think they still have time to change everything.*) He was panicking, searching, panicking more. And because Gwyn wanted to believe that was what was happening, she suggested that they go into therapy, couples counseling. So she could try to understand. But Thomas was against this. Therapy. Understanding.

This isn't a simple infidelity. That was what he said. That was his answer to her request. *This is who I am now. It is what I want my life to mean.*

He wasn't interested in helping Gwyn understand. It was a total lifestyle change and she could accept it or—if she thought he was turning into someone she didn't recognize—she could choose something else for herself. But either way, this was the direction he was choosing.

No place to meet in the middle. An open and shut case. Either she was in or out.

With such a halfhearted invitation, he certainly didn't count on her choosing in. He didn't count on Gywn's reaching deep into herself, the part that wasn't sure how she felt about any religion, especially one that she knew so little about, and deciding that what she believed in was her husband. The one she married thirty-five years ago, in the very house they still shared. He didn't count on her summoning up how she had felt then, and driving to Oyster Bay, to the Buddhist Center to join her husband for Thursday meditation class: Gwyn walking through the peaceful hallways in a red dress, black scarf wrapped around her neck. As if it were something she knew how to do. Pray, learn, change. As if it were something she could figure out how to do.

A woman in a long, dark robe introduced herself as one of the center's master teachers, *please call me Donna,* and asked Gwyn how she could help her. "I am looking for tonight's meditation class," she said. "I am meeting my husband, Thomas Huntington."

"The meditation class is in the third room on the right, but did you say your husband was Thomas? I'm sorry, but there is no one in the class by that name."

"Are you certain? How many people are there? Maybe you missed him."

"Five."

Gwyn shook her head, blinking in confusion. "But he is in the middle of your sixteen-week meditation class."

"Is it possible that he registered under a different name?"

Maybe. Maybe he thought they would know his financial situation if he used his real name. Maybe that would be looked down upon. So Gwyn walked the rest of the way down the hall anyway, to look inside the room herself. They were on the floor—the five. Three men and two women. Three brunettes, one blonde, one gray. All in brown robes, all silently kneeling over brown benches.

Thomas was nowhere. She went back out into her car, and stared at herself in her rearview mirror for an hour, maybe longer. As if her own face would show Thomas's secret, or show her where to go next. It didn't. She had no idea where to look. Not that night. But she knew the beginning of the truth. She knew what was really happening with her husband.

It was another woman.

With blue eyes and noble hips, a tattoo of the Chinese

character for peace on the nape of her neck, the one for joy on one of those hips. Her thirtieth birthday still years away.

It is still the other woman. And because she has refused to tell Thomas that she knows this, Gwyn has been left in the tricky position of putting together the rest of it—painfully putting together what she has wanted to know least—why Thomas has lied to her, why he has lied so elaborately.

Because the truth was so simple. An affair with a younger woman? How absurd! How cliché! But how familiar, too. If Thomas confessed there was someone else—as opposed to making up the Buddhism story—Gwyn would have been furious, but so furious that she would have wanted out of the marriage? Hard to say. Many friends have dealt with infidelity and survived. She might have chosen to do what they chose to do: to stay and to fight. For their marriages. For their husbands. For the only life they knew.

But religious conversion? Newfound belief?

Thomas was banking on this making him seem like a stranger to Gwyn. And who wants to fight to stay with a stranger? Who wants to stay?

This is why he lied, Gwyn knows. She knows now. She knows all of it: Thomas didn't want her to fight. He didn't want her to blame him, or feel hurt. He didn't want to be the bad guy. He just wanted to leave.

This isn't a simple infidelity, he had said. How right he had been. And how wrong.

Gwyn takes a final drag and puts out the joint with her thumb and index finger. A quick tap of the base. And puts the rest back in the walnut box, slides it under the sink. Then she wets her fingers, runs them along the bridge of her nose. Steadies herself.

He still doesn't know that she knows the truth. Because he underestimated Gwyn in the worst way. He underestimated the great lengths she would go to to try to understand him. To try to meet him wherever he needed to go.

He underestimated how much she loved him.

So now, on the eve of their thirty-fifth anniversary, he isn't the only one with something he is trying to hide. And Gwyn won't be the only one asking the question: Can you ever know anyone?

Maitri.

Forgiveness.

No.

Not tonight.

part two   *unexpected guests*

Maggie

They are having a divorce party.

They are having a divorce party. Maggie knew this coming in. She knew most of this coming in. And yet, to hear them talk about the actual event, to have the event be this close to them, makes it feel more immediate. And certainly more bizarre. Everything here feels bizarre. Beneath these hardwood floors, soft curtains. Beneath these enormous windows looking out over the ocean and the clouds and the rest of everything.

And still. A small, arguably reasonable voice enters into her head, asks a question she is not sure she wants to answer—*Who are you to judge? Why would you even want to?*

Maggie was nine years old when her mother left them. There was nothing like a party—nothing like an announcement, even. Maybe Maggie would have been better off with some kind of ceremony. But her mother simply walked out the door on an otherwise typical Tuesday night, and no one even told Maggie it happened. For the first couple of weeks, her father pretended Jen Lyons Mackenzie (age twenty-nine, landscape architect, Aries) had gone on a trip—an extended vacation back out to Eugene to visit her parents. Maybe Eli was hoping it would turn out to be true, or true enough. That, at the panic-inducing age of twenty-nine, Jen had been rash in her decision to depart, would come to her senses and come back to them. But what kind of judgment was Eli using, hiding the reality? Her father was trying to save Maggie, by choosing which pieces of the truth she got to see. Which was the surest way to never save anyone.

She hoists her bag higher on her shoulder, follows Nate up the stairs, toward his childhood bedroom, and tries not to focus on how today is starting to feel like that. A day of hidden truths: incredible finances, childhood friends, creepy two-hundred-person parties.

Instead, she focuses on the several black-and-white photographs lining the staircase. There are gorgeous photos of the family, and enormous landscape photographs, mostly of Montauk—though, not surprisingly, she is mostly drawn to the ones with Nate in them. But then her eyes catch on the one at the very top of the stairs, a large eight-by-ten: Gwyn and Thomas in the front seat of an old pickup truck, the highway behind them, Thomas's arm straight out in a way that suggests to Maggie that he is the one shooting the photo. Gwyn, meanwhile, is kissing his neck. And he is laughing. He is really laughing.

Maggie stops in front of it, runs her finger along the black frame. It is a nice picture, but when she looks up to ask Nate about it, he is not there. He has gone on ahead, without her, which is her first real indication that he may actually be affected by what he's heard in the living room.

He's left his bedroom door open for her. It is a corner room, small, with wood planks lining the walls and a square window near the ceiling that is the only source of light. It looks like a boat cabin, in its way, covered with too much blue: blue comforter and carpet. Blue bike in the corner. She goes right to it—the bike—runs her hands along the seat.

"This was your room?" she says.

He nods. "This was my room."

Nate is sitting on the edge of the bed, and she goes to sit down next to him. His T-shirt is hiked above his waist, and she can see the hair there leading downward from his belly button. She moves toward him, reaches out to touch him there.

Her eyes focus on the bulletin board above his desk: newspaper clippings and ribbons, lots of empty tacks where things used to be, things that are long gone now. She wants to tell him she likes his room, but he tenses, even at her touch, and she can feel that he is annoyed—or maybe embarrassed, or maybe both. It isn't exactly about her, and yet she doesn't say anything, takes her hand away.

"We don't have to talk about it, Nate," she says.

"You obviously want to."

She takes a deep breath in. "I just want to make sure you're doing okay," she says.

Nate is quiet. "I'm fine," he says.

"I can tell."

"Mag, I can understand that you are freaked out. I get that. If this were your parents' house, and I walked into all of this, I think I'd freak out a little too."

When it was her dad's house they were visiting, Maggie had been so worried that her father would drink too much, say something inappropriate. The worst thing he did was speak with *a little* too much detail about his most recent girlfriend, Melinda. And yet it had been tame in comparison to Maggie's fears, hadn't it? Maybe because Maggie had told Nate everything about her father a long time before they went to Asheville. He knew her whole story—everything that could potentially cause friction— and so, when it all went well enough, it created a sense of relief.

"If this were my parents' house, you'd deal," she says.

"So you're dealing?" he said.

She shrugs. "You're a better person than me."

She is trying to make a joke—to bring him back to her—and it works for a second. He smiles. Then his smile disappears. "Please don't feel weird. This is all fine. This is what they want. I accept that. Sometimes things just don't work out. Sometimes, it's easier to separate . . ."

She looks at him, worrying that he's missing it—the bigger picture—and wondering if he is missing it for his parents' sake, or if he would also be capable of missing it for them. "Something just feels off about it," she says. "The divorce party. I think something else is going on."

"What are you talking about?" he says.

"I'm not sure yet," she says. "I'm not sure I can explain it. I just have a bad feeling."

"A bad feeling?"

"Yes. I have a feeling that it is not as simple as them both wanting this."

He looks down at her hand, turning it over. There is no engagement ring there. She hadn't wanted one. Now she almost wishes she had one. She wishes she had something to look down at, as proof that they promised to be in this together. Because, right now, she is feeling outside of it, of them.

"I'm sorry," he says.

"For what?"

"For putting us here."

Maggie shakes her head, trying to take this out of the realm of the two of them. *This is Nate's family's weirdness, not his.* Nate has always worked hard, so hard to be good to her, to be there for her. It is unfair to even worry in her own mind, now, about whether that will be the case. Because of his parents? Because of anything he says about why they've chosen to end things?

"I'm the one that should be sorry," she says. "It's your family. You know them better than I do, and I shouldn't be rushing to judgment." She makes herself meet his eyes. "I just feel a little overwhelmed by everything . . ."

But suddenly she doesn't want to say even to herself what the everything is. The part of him that she is seeing now too. It has taken Georgia to point out that Nate gets absent, doesn't want to deal. How could Maggie not have picked up on that before now? Has she not noticed? Or has she been too scared to acknowledge that she has and what it may mean?

"You know," he says, "let's just lie down for a while . . . take our clothes off for a while." He smiles at her. "If we get some sleep, this will all feel less weird. Plus when we wake up, we'll be that much closer to out of here. Sound like a good plan?"

She nods. "Sounds good."

But just as they are lying back, there is a knock on the door. "Nate!" It's Georgia. She's knocking more while she's talking. "Can you come downstairs with me for a minute? I need to talk to you. And don't pretend you can't hear me. I'll bust this door down and make you hear me."

"I need a minute, Georgia."

"No." She knocks again. "*Now.*"

Maggie touches his knee, shrugs. "Go. It's fine. I'll sleep for a little while. It will be good. You can talk to your family without worrying about me."

He turns back toward Maggie, putting his forehead against hers—holding it there, closing his eyes.

"I'll be back."

"I'll be here."

He nods, pulling back, and kissing her on top of her head, which she imagines is supposed to bring her calm, but has the opposite effect. Because it feels nothing like him.

Maggie listens to the door click shut, and looks back over at the bulletin board, at the red ribbons in the middle, and the newspaper clippings again, and the empty tacks. There are no photos up there anymore. But she thinks of the last one on the staircase: the one of Gwyn and Thomas in the pickup truck. They look in love in that picture. They look very much in love. How do you get from there to here? Does it start with one lie, one small omission? One conversation that you need to have, and can't seem to?

Which is when the door opens again. It's Nate.

"Can I tell you something I've never told you before?" he says. And he looks at her, really looks at her, until she holds his gaze for a second, sees him. "I like you more than anyone," he says.

She smiles at him. "I like you more than anyone," she says.

But then—just when she needs him to stay most, and can ask for it least—he is gone again.

Gwyn

She started to get to this earlier: the billion-dollar industries. The ones that survive based on the faulty idea that women like her have, the idea that if you keep yourself beautiful, that if you keep yourself looking a certain way, you are safe. In your life, in your marriage, in yourself. How many times has she heard a friend talking about someone leaving his wife and saying, *well, she really let herself go*? The implication being that it is less his fault than hers, that he can't be expected to stay for someone who is less than perfect.

Only, what if you stay perfect? And he leaves you anyway? Who are you going to blame it on, then? Especially when this other person, the one he is leaving for, isn't beautiful? When she isn't anything like the person you're supposed to try hard—try with everything you have—to keep being?

This is the worst position of all, Gwyn thinks. She has stayed beautiful, and it hasn't saved her from anything. In fact, it may have left her more vulnerable, because it allowed her to get complacent. Thomas still stared at her as she walked into a room, touched the small of her back, still told her she had the most perfect hips and shoulders and breasts he'd ever seen. She let those things mean something. She let them stand in place of the things he rarely said enough, like: *I adore you, and I always have*.

She straightens her dress out, leaves the bathroom, and heads down the stairs toward the kitchen. If she can spend some time in the kitchen without being harassed, without see-ing anyone, it will be no small miracle. She wants to start bak-ing the cake. She wants to be left alone.

But she turns on the kitchen light and it reveals both of her children, in the dark, just where she guessed she'd find them: Nate sitting on a stool by the counter, Georgia leaning against the countertop itself. The ingredients for the cake are pushed to the side. Shortening and cocoa and sugar. Beets and fresh but-termilk, too many eggs. Gwyn closes her eyes, opens them, hop-ing to see something else. They could be ten or fifteen as easily as the grown people that are sitting in front of her now: Nate bending into his shoulders, Georgia leaning backward on her tiny elbows. Anyone who says people *change* should ask a mother. She can tell you that her children—in the ways that count most—are exactly as they've always been.

"You're going to have to move," she says, tapping Georgia on her cheek.

Georgia stays where she is. "We've been talking about it, Mom," she says, "and if this divorce party is some twisted at-tempt to make us feel better, then we feel fine, okay? We'll feel a lot better without it."

Gwyn reaches around Georgia for the eggs, the butter. She reaches around her daughter, and starts to get organized. "It's too late to cancel. Everyone has been invited."

"*Everyone has been invited?* You sound British," Georgia says.

She looks at her daughter disapprovingly.

"Do they even know what they've been invited to?" she asks. "Do they even know what tonight is really about?"

How can Gwyn answer that? She nods, because *yes* is the closest thing to the correct answer. Her friends do know they've been invited to a divorce party, and they do know the gist of the rest of it: that she and Thomas are splitting. They don't know there is another woman, though. They probably wouldn't believe it if Gwyn told them, wouldn't want to believe it, which is really beside the point. Because she can't tell them anyway. She can't bear to hear them say what they'll inevitably say—*Thomas is going to come running back to you.* She can't hear them say it, then have to find out how wrong they are about that too.

"So just that we are clear," Georgia says, folding her arms across her chest, "putting a pretty face on our family's demise in front of everyone we know is the healthiest way to go. What kind of parenting is that? Do you know what my therapist is going to say?"

She squeezes Georgia's elbow. "You can tell your therapist that your father and I decided together, with *our therapist,* that celebrating our family, one last time, is the healthiest way to go."

"You guys have a therapist?"

"No. But will you tell your therapist that we do? It makes us sound better."

"Mom, this isn't funny."

"Well, it's a little funny."

She looks at her daughter, who looks very upset—though, Gwyn guesses, not exactly for the reasons she is saying. Yes, it must be hard for her to think of her parents separating. Gwyn imagines that it is particularly hard for her right now when she doesn't want to think about anyone separating. When she has to deal with the fact that her family is constantly worried her relationship may be next.

"You know what? Please don't be so transparent, Mother. I see that look in your eyes. This has nothing to do with me and Denis, or me being worried about Denis and me, or whatever else you think that I'm putting on you and Dad. We're fine. *We're great.*"

Gwyn puts up her hands in surrender. "I'm just trying to explain that tonight is a *nice* thing. There's a reason divorce parties are getting popular around here. We've gone to three this year alone. There's another later this month, Syril and Maureen Livingston, you know the screenwriter couple from up the block?" She directs this question to Nate. "They wrote that terrible love-on-a-plane heist film a few years back. Anyway, they had a beautiful one, and said that it made it a lot easier for their twins to come to terms with their decision, to feel good about it."

"Aren't their twins six years old?" Georgia says.

"And?" Gwyn says.

Georgia pushes away from the countertop. "I'm going to lie down," she says. "Before I say something I'll regret." She pats her brother on the shoulder. "You try."

"I'm on it," Nate says, but he looks distracted.

"Wait," Gwyn says.

Georgia starts to leave, but Gwyn hands her the pile of divorce literature, which has made its way into the kitchen. She puts *Loving Divorce* on the top—the best book she has found about all of this.

She has dog-eared the chapter about divorce parties, why they are a good idea, how they help a family heal. How, if done right, they help a family appreciate that there are *many forms of love, many forms of staying together, even if apart.*

"Excellent," Georgia says. "Are we done here?"

Gwyn nods. "If you want to be," she says. And she watches her daughter go—her daughter, who, from the back, doesn't look at all pregnant, doesn't look at all different from how she's always been.

"So," she says, turning back to Nate. "Do you hate me too?"

Nate looks at her. "No."

She puts on her apron, reaches under the kitchen sink for her biggest mixing bowl, its matching oversize spoon. "Well, that's something," she says.

"Though I can't help but think you shouldn't have let me bring Maggie here for the first time during all of this, Mom. This is a lot for someone to walk into."

She puts the spoon down. "You knew we were having this party. You even knew how big it was going to be."

"I wasn't thinking what that meant."

"And whose fault is that?"

Nate is quiet. "Maybe mine."

Gwyn moves the ingredients around the bowl, takes out the ripped, yellowed recipe—marked RED VELV on top in marker—as if she needs the recipe, as if she doesn't know it by heart. She looks up at her son. "I didn't want that," she says.

"Which part?"

"The part that makes you uncomfortable. I don't want that. You know I don't."

He runs his hand through his hair, the way he does when he is trying to make sense of things—seven-year-old Nate, thirty-three-year-old Nate—and then, with a small smile, he gets off the stool and goes to the sink and starts washing his hands. He dries them on his own jeans, turning back toward the countertop, untying the shortening bag. He dumps three cups into the bowl, chef eyes it as close enough, and starts looking for the coconut extract to create the puddle in the middle of it.

"What are you doing?" she says.

"What do you think?"

He is helping her. That's what she thinks. He is helping her now, and he is always going to help her—seven-year-old Nate, thirty-three-year-old Nate—if she gives him the choice. It warms her, and makes her feel something else too. Something like pride. Who wants to hear about that, though? He doesn't. He doesn't want to hear her say any of that right now.

So, instead, she rubs his back, and hands over the black bottle of extract from the spice rack. Its small cap, loose.

"Thank you, baby," she says, as he takes it.

"Don't mention it."

She leans toward him, as he adds the lemon zest, her secret ingredient, the way she showed him a long time ago, the way he has remembered to do.

"And you guys are going to be fine," she says.

"Me and Georgia?"

"You and Maggie. People don't break up because someone's family is a little . . . *messy*. If that were the case, no one would ever get married." She touches his jaw. "But I am sorry. Have I said that yet? I'm sorry if I caught her off-guard. I'm sorry if I caused any strife."

He shakes his head, cracks open an egg. "The truth is that I managed to freak her out all by myself about sixty minutes before we came here. I waited until this morning to tell her some things that I should have told her about before now."

"Like what?"

Nate doesn't answer at first, reaching forward and plugging

in the mixer, holding it over the bowl, slowly running it through the mixture.

"I didn't tell her much about how I grew up," he says. "Or, I should say, I didn't tell her everything. I didn't really tell her about the finances, for starters."

Gwyn unplugs it. "One more time?"

"It never seemed like the right time to tell her." He looks at Gwyn, meets her eyes. "It feels so separate from my life. From *our* life."

"Nate, *your life* is that you are opening a restaurant together. And she had a right to know. . . . Not that you were going to take any money for it from us, after last time. You made that much clear. But you should have explained that part to her. My God, she must feel so confused."

"I can see that now."

He starts to mix again, but she puts her hands over his, tries to make him listen to her. "You have nothing to be ashamed of."

"I know that."

"I don't think you do."

He looks at her. He is silent, as if considering it for a minute, whether to say what she can already see on his face. The worst part.

"The thing is that she doesn't know about the last time."

Gwyn can feel her jaw drop in disbelief, can feel her disbelief running through her—and something like anger. Because he looks in this moment—she sees it in him—like his father. She usually sees pieces of his grandfather, Champ, in him. But now, it is Thomas she sees. Those sweet but put-upon eyes, that reluctant frown. And now it scares her.

"You haven't told her, Nate?"

"I wanted to." He clears his throat. "But she was already so freaked out that I didn't tell her about the money situation, and then we saw Murph on the bus. I think learning another secret of this magnitude now would be a lot for anyone to take."

"And what? This morning is the first time the two of you have ever had a conversation?"

"Apparently."

He pulls the food coloring out of its box, puts several drops into the bowl, stirring it into the mixture. And refusing to do it, refusing to look at her, which tells her more than she wants to know.

She shakes her head. How can she explain it so he will hear her? He needs to tell Maggie *now*. Because if she finds out about Ryan another way, it will make the rest of it, anything else he hasn't told her, seem bigger, and also pale in comparison.

"I'm going to tell her, Mom. I will. I'll tell her as soon as we get back to Brooklyn, as soon as this weekend is behind us . . . I'll tell her the rest of the story."

It's not a story, she wants to tell her son. *It's your life.*

"You need to promise me. Not that I'm the person you need to be promising, but I'm going to have to do—"

"I will, I am planning to, as soon as she can hear it," he says, wiping his hands on a dishtowel, as if that solves it. "But while we are being all honest here, then let me ask you something."

She turns on the oven, letting it heat. "Shoot," she says.

"Are you sure this is what you want?"

She feels herself go stiff. "The party or the divorce?"

"Either, both. I know I'm probably supposed to have my own reaction to it, but the reaction I'm honestly having now is that it's okay with me. If it's really what you want."

She meets his eyes, holds them, making herself believe it so she can say it. "Yes, this is really what I want."

"Then why are you still making his favorite cake?"

She looks down at the now-messy countertop, the dirtied dishes and bowls and spoons in the kitchen sink. She wipes her fingers on her apron, the fronts of them, then the back.

"I don't know," she says.

He nods. "Because truthfully, Mom, Maggie thinks there is something else going on. And normally I would argue, but I don't know . . ." He pauses. "You just don't seem like yourself."

Then, as if the conversation is over—and she guesses it is, for now—he turns away from her to get the ingredients for the frosting. And she begins to pour the cake into its container. Where it will bake. Where it will complete itself.

"Now that is the nicest thing anyone has said to me all day," she says.

Maggie

It's not that she is convinced she would have fallen asleep, but she was close to it, closer than she's been in a few days: lying on top of Nate's bed, her eyes closing, her mind in that silent place right before sleep. She wishes she had gotten there from a place of relaxation, but this is more from the opposite. It is more from not wanting to acknowledge what she is feeling in her stomach, what she worries is going on around her.

Then Georgia knocks on the door. The first time, jarring Maggie. The second time, giving her no choice but to respond.

"Maggie! Can I come in?" Georgia says, as she opens the door, answers her own question with a yes. "Were you sleeping?"

"Not exactly," she says.

Georgia enters: a book under her arm, holding a bottle of absinthe, a thin shot glass. She gets on the bed, lying down. Then she hands Maggie the absinthe and the glass.

"I brought you a snack," she says.

Maggie looks at her, then down at the bottle, unscrewing the cap. The pungent smell that comes out is a mix of apples and cherries and licorice and wood. Maggie remembers trying to buy a bottle of this for Nate out in San Francisco the day he gave notice at the restaurant and they decided for certain to open their own place in New York. He had told her that he loved absinthe, but she went to every liquor store she could think of and could only find imitations, the real version illegal and unavailable anywhere in the continental United States.

"It's the real absinthe?" she asks Georgia now.

Georgia nods. "Denis smuggled it in from Canada."

"Is absinthe legal in Canada?"

"Oh, how should I know?"

She opens the book, which Maggie recognizes from Gwyn's pile downstairs—*Graceful Divorce* is written on the cover, above a purposely blurry photograph of two hands, separating from each other. Georgia flips through pages until she stops on one, her fingers skimming a passage. "Listen to this," she says, and begins to read:

> *The purpose of the parting ritual is to replace animosity with harmony. It is a message that closing the door on marriage does not mean closing the door on the love you feel for each other. It is a message that wherever your lives may take the two of you from this point forward, you will remain connected in your hearts. . . .*

"Gross," Maggie says. "What is that?"

"Apparently, what we have to look forward to tonight." She pauses. "Set to orchestra music."

Maggie pours some of the thick drink into a shot glass, downs it, pours herself a little more, downs it again.

"There we go!" Georgia says, and starts to applaud.

Maggie's throat starts burning, her eyes tearing up. "That is strong."

"Stop trying to make me jealous."

Maggie looks down at her empty shot glass. When she was searching for this for Nate, a store clerk told her it was banned because it could make you crazy. How long does that take? It is starting to feel like she is going quietly crazy anyway, but it would be nice to have the alcohol to blame it on. She hasn't eaten yet today, nothing except the popcorn. She is hungry, specifically hungry, wants ginger pancakes. She tries hard to crave something else, knowing that it means she is in trouble. As a little girl, whenever she was about to get sick, or she would sense disaster striking, her craving for them would rise up, like a bright red hazard sign. She thinks it has something to do with one of her clearest memories of her mother—the two of them sitting on Maggie's bed, early one Saturday morning, eating ginger pancakes and drinking unsweetened iced tea. Listening to the radio. She can still call it up whenever she eats the pancakes. Not just the memory. But the feeling, as if it is happening right now.

"Can I ask you something personal?" Georgia says.

Maggie turns her body so she is completely facing Georgia. "Of course."

Georgia looks at Maggie, then back up at the ceiling. "I'm having a little girl," she says. "I found out yesterday."

"Oh my God, Georgia!" Maggie touches her arm. "That's amazing."

Georgia nods. "You're the only one who knows." She pauses, rubbing her belly. "You're the only one that knows, including Denis."

Which is when Maggie remembers how this started. "And what's the question?"

"Do I have to tell him?"

"Why wouldn't you tell him?"

"Denis really wanted a boy. I didn't care, as long as the baby is healthy, but Denis did, and I found out because I wanted to surprise him, if it were a boy. Now that it's not, I am worried."

"Worried about what?"

"That he won't be happy. That he'll be disappointed and unable to hide it."

Maggie looks over at Georgia, trying to think of how to calm her nerves, trying to calm her. "I'm sure he is going to be thrilled. When that baby comes into the world, it will be the only baby he wants."

"How do you know?"

"I think that's just the way it works."

She smiles, uncertain. "In the movies?" she says.

"And television," Maggie says.

Georgia's smile gets bigger, starts to light up her face, just as Maggie hears a loud vibrating noise, and Georgia pulls her cell phone out of her jeans pocket. She holds out the phone so Maggie can see DENIS on the caller ID. Then she flips her feet over the side of the bed and sits up, so she can answer.

"Hey, baby," she says. "Where are you? Please tell me that you are at the airport, getting on the plane."

From the expression on Georgia's face, which goes immediately back from happy to far less so, it is clear that, wherever Denis is, it is not at the airport getting on the plane.

Georgia gets up and Maggie thinks she is going to leave the room, but she goes into the closet, closing the door behind her. Maggie looks down at the shot glass in her hand, trying not to listen to Georgia's voice, which is getting increasingly louder.

And suddenly, the closet door is open and Georgia is standing there, no cell phone in her hand.

"I don't want to talk about it," she says.

Maggie nods. "Okay."

She looks pissed and for a second she thinks Georgia is going to take the absinthe bottle and down the whole thing. But she doesn't. She just gets real close to Maggie.

"Let's get out of here," she says.

"Where to?"

"You'll love it."

The last thing Maggie wants to do is go anywhere, even somewhere she'll love. She wants to let the alcohol work its magic. She wants it to make her tired. She wants to sleep. But it makes Georgia look alive, the thought of getting out of here, and Maggie can't handle stopping that. So she takes a deep breath. "Can I bring the absinthe?"

"I think we can make room."

She ignores the spinning in her head as she starts to stand. "Then let's go," she says.

Gwyn

She is washing the dishes when Thomas comes into the kitchen in his wet suit, his surfboard in his hand. This isn't an anomaly. It is his pattern: most afternoons, when he gets home from work, he goes for a run along the ocean's edge, and, depending on the tide, he goes surfing. Sometimes, after, he also goes for a bike ride, even in the rain, even in the snow: anything to get outside for a while, get active. It was years into their marriage before Gwyn accepted that it was impossible to talk with him about important things—about anything, really—before he had that time alone, outside, to decompress. He was in a much better mood afterward, his face more open, accepting. In the space between work and the time he spent outside, she could have the best news in the world for him, and he wasn't able to engage her, or hear it.

Thomas opens the oven, takes a look at the cake, the thick butter smell wafting through the air. "Is that red velvet cake?"

Gwyn flicks water at him. "Close it. It's bad luck."

"How do you figure?"

"You know how it's bad luck to see the bride in the wedding gown before the wedding?"

"It's bad luck to see the red velvet cake before the divorce party?"

"Exactly."

He smiles, doing what she says, closing the oven tight. "I'll take your word for it."

She turns the water on stronger as he leans the surfboard against the wall, opening the refrigerator door, searching for a bottle of green tea to bring. She knows that is what he wants and says, "Second shelf."

He bends to grab it. "I think the kids are okay with our plans for tonight," he says. "We knew they wouldn't be happy about the size, but it seems okay with them."

"Really? You think so?"

Maybe she expects him to be mad at her, mad that she was fairly passive-aggressive during the conversation with their children—that she didn't rise to the occasion the way she had said she would, been as smooth about it as she could have been. He doesn't seem mad at all, though, which is almost worse. It feels like just another reminder that he barely sees her anymore.

He closes the fridge door, shakes the tea bottle in his left hand. "Georgia was upset," he says. "But she'll calm down."

"We can hope."

"Gwyn," he says. "I think it's hard for them to see us together. It will get better after a while."

She looks up from her dishes. "How's that, Thomas?"

"They'll realize that we aren't supposed to stay that way."

She nods—trying to ignore the tightening in her chest—as he moves toward the other side of the sink, reaches toward the windowsill to turn on the small radio they keep there. "I just want to get the weather before I head out," he says, tuning in to 1010, just as the weatherman is finishing up his report:

. . . Expect thunderstorms in early evening, growing in intensity throughout the night. Certainly not a repeat of the hurricane that greeted us back in 1938, on this very day, but certainly not the time to go walking along the beach.

"That's not great for tonight," Thomas says. He pulls off the bottle cap, takes a sip. "But I think we'll be okay. The barn can handle it, right? I don't think we should worry."

That's fine with her. With everything else she is trying to handle for this evening, the weather is the last thing she is going to concern herself with.

"Do you know how many times my father told me what happened to him during the hurricane?"

Do you know how many times you've told me? she wants to say. She could repeat the whole thing by heart, even what happened to them afterward: Champ fondly remembering how the town of Montauk got rebuilt in the aftermath, how he and Anna got involved in resurrecting this area from what it had faced.

"It was because of the hurricane that they decided to stay out here full time," Thomas says. "Most people didn't do that back then, didn't consider that as an option. It's weird to think about it, how they would have had a totally different life otherwise."

She smiles, but she doesn't feel like talking about Champ and Anna. It makes her miss them, makes her wish they were here. If they were, she can't help but think that Thomas wouldn't be doing what he is doing. She knows this, at least, he would be doing it differently.

Gwyn motions out the window to where Nate is standing near the edge of the cliff, by the swing, throwing rocks out at the ocean.

"Why don't you ask him to go with you?" she says, motioning toward their son. "Maggie's upstairs in his room sleeping. And it will be good for you to talk to him while you have some time alone. It will be good for you to get him to talk."

"About what?" Thomas looks confused. "About you and me?"

Gwyn gives him a look. "About him and Maggie. About why he is choosing not to tell her some very important things."

"Like what?"

"Like she doesn't know about his first restaurant."

"What are you talking about? How can she not know about that? That's insane."

Is it? she wants to say. *What about all the things you think I don't know about? Is that insane too?*

"What did he say exactly?"

Gwyn takes a breath in, not in the mood to translate, not in the mood to go through it again—the little that Nate told her, the rest that she couldn't seem to pry from him over one cake-baking session. "Just ask him, Thomas," she says, her anger rising. "Ask him what he is doing."

"Okay," he says, and he picks his surfboard up. "Except Maggie's not upstairs. She just went out with Georgia a little while ago. I heard the car pull out. They didn't come in here and tell you?"

"No, I didn't even hear them leave." She puts the sponge down. "That's odd. Well, I'll let her know. I'll let her know, and I'll keep her busy."

He taps her on the nose, makes a quick circle there. "You doing okay?" he says.

She feels herself cringe at his touch, at how it feels when he moves away. "Sure," she says. "I'm doing *great*."

"Gwyn—"

"Get going. Come on. Before it starts to rain."

He points at the radio. "It sounds like we have hours before any of that hits us."

"The one thing we do *not* have before any of that hits us, Thomas, is hours," she says and he gives her a look, but he picks up his surfboard and leaves.

Gwyn takes her time. She finishes with the dishes, puts them back in the cupboard, and calmly heads outside herself, but in the opposite way from Nate and Thomas. She heads down her driveway toward their nearest neighbor's place. It is quiet out here, silent almost, but soon enough, they will be coming to set it up: the barn being transformed in one swoop, candelas covering the now pushed-to-the-side tables. A buffet of food circling the center. The rafters coated with white balloons and glass balls.

Still, she has a little longer to get this last piece together. And she's come this far, but she's not nervous now. She's not. She is just letting herself know what she knows, like a mantra she's been repeating since all of Thomas's lies started: *More than one thing is never true.* People love to say the opposite, love to talk about inner conflict, nuances, levels of complication. But if this last year has taught her anything, it has taught her that people are clearer on what they want than they admit to themselves. They want something, or they don't. They decide to keep working at a relationship or they give up. They love someone or they love someone else. And if they love someone else, it is often the idea that they love most, especially when they haven't learned enough to figure out that this new person probably won't save them either.

Thomas hasn't learned that yet, which is why he can lie and call the girl religion. And why Gwyn is left to call her new religion the girl. Following the girl. Learning from her. Learning about who her husband has decided he wants to be. Learning about what is coming next for her family.

And here it is. What is coming next.

Here she is.

Sitting on the back steps at the Buckleys'.

Her husband's mistress. In a large jacket and frayed jeans, two low-flying braids against the side of her head. Her eyes darting back and forth, looking nervous—holding a large silver tray of oversize mushroom caps.

"Eve," Gwyn says, and moves toward her. "Welcome."

Maggie

This is what Maggie knew about the lighthouse out on Montauk Point, before she actually went to the lighthouse out on Montauk Point: that it was the oldest lighthouse in America, around for over two hundred years, and still used to help navigate ships in and out on the tip of Long Island, this important port on the edge of the world. What she didn't know, until today, is that many couples get married here, that it's booked years in advance, so that on any given weekend, a bride and a groom can say their vows in front of fifty friends, the ocean in the background, the lighthouse up on the hill to the right, like a beacon shining, eternal. Something for the minister to point to as emblematic of the union, of what the couple has to come.

When she and Georgia pulled up, a wedding was in progress, and so they swung around to a private "lot" that Georgia knew about—more like an unused dirt road—and Maggie followed Georgia through the forest until they reached the rocks, a small beach area just beyond—marked GOVERNMENT PROPERTY: NO TRESPASSING—where they could watch the ceremony, undetected.

"Are you sure we should be here?" Maggie asks.

"Shhh!" Georgia says, pointing to the couple forty yards away. "I'm concentrating."

From where Maggie sits with Georgia on these rocks, she can see everything, and hear nothing, and make up whatever story she wants. From here the couple getting married can be anyone.

This couple does seem to be older, in their seventies—if Maggie is guessing correctly—and this is probably why they are including readings and scripture and more readings. They probably want to include the people from their previous lives—all of their kids, all of their kids' kids—and make them feel a part of this. There also seem to be a lot of musicians, taking turns playing music, singing songs, throughout the ceremony. Probably one of them is a musician, or both, and this is how they met. Or, at least, this is what Maggie decides.

"I used to always think I'd get married here," Georgia says. "I was dating this hedge-fund dude when I was just out of college who liked me because I was just out of college, and I reserved this place for a June wedding. I almost forgot to cancel in time. I almost forgot I couldn't stand him, and so should probably get my deposit back."

Maggie turns toward her, and tries to focus on what she is saying. *Did all of that make sense?* She looks down at the absinthe bottle, and the too-big dent she has made in it. And maybe it is because she is sitting down that she can't feel it exactly, how too-big the dent actually is. Somewhere inside, though, she knows it is happening. She knows it and isn't doing anything to stop it.

"When I was growing up, my mom and I would come up here sometimes on Saturdays and watch the weddings. I was always so amazed when the couple actually went through with the thing. That no one got up and walked away, changed his mind at the last minute. I think I was always waiting for that. Isn't that terrible? A whole life ruined for my amusement."

"Sounds pretty human," Maggie says.

"Maybe."

She looks at Georgia more carefully. "Do you and Denis not talk about getting married?"

That is certainly the absinthe talking. This sounds like something she would be too afraid to ask normally, if she were thinking clearly about it.

Georgia shakes her head, slowly. "No, Denis wants to wait until after the baby comes."

"To get married?"

"To talk about it."

Georgia reaches over and takes the bottle of absinthe from Maggie. She takes a long smell of it, and then hands the bottle back.

"Have you ever heard that Oscar Wilde saying? 'All women become their mothers.' I think it was Oscar Wilde. You know the quote, right? 'All women become their mothers. That is their tragedy . . .'"

Maggie feels it, a familiar pang rising up in her chest. At even the sound of the word *mother,* at a reminder of what she never really had. Should it be like this twenty-plus years since her exit? Does the *should* even matter? It is this way, and there is no denying it. Maggie's mother left and never came back and Maggie never did anything to find her. Or to let her go. And maybe this has made some sort of difference she is afraid to look at.

"I've been thinking about that recently," Georgia says. "I love my mom, but I've been worrying a little that it's true." She looks at Maggie. "You think it is?"

Maggie shakes her head. If we are bound to become our mothers, Maggie knows, then she is bound to leave the people who love her most. She will decide it is too tough or too uncomfortable or too involved, and go. Hasn't this been what she has always done? It has been. She has always been the one to leave, to find reasons not to stay—her chosen career and all its built-in reasons—even when the men she's been with have given her many chances not to look for them.

"God I hope not," she says.

"Me too, but I think it was always hard for him to connect. We kind of all accepted that about him. That was just who he was. He needed a certain amount of time alone, time to feel like he wasn't being locked in by us. And my mom was always protecting him, you know? She was always giving him that."

It takes Maggie a minute to realize that Georgia is talking about Thomas. That she is talking about how her mother and her father used to be together, how that used to look to her.

"The part that bothers me is that my mother would do it without even thinking about it. She has never been good at taking her own space, getting her own needs met, but she has no problem saying 'your dad needs *xyz*.' Like it was her job to make us understand him. Not his." She pauses. "I just don't want to be the one."

"Which one?"

"The one who is always trying harder."

Maggie looks over at Georgia, who is coming out blurry. She is blurry from Maggie's bad attempt to focus too hard or her absinthe-filled mind or both. She takes a deep breath in, blinking hard, and looks up at the sky, the blue giving way to something darker.

"Are you afraid that you are?" Maggie says. "The one who tries harder?"

"No," she says. "I'm just afraid that my family thinks I am."

Maggie looks at her, confused. "What's the difference what they think?"

"I'm afraid they'll convince me."

Maggie holds up the bottle, pours Georgia a quarter of a shot into the shot glass—not even really a quarter, more like a teaspoon. And she holds it up, like an answer. Then she hands it over.

Georgia downs it. "Man, I knew you would make me feel better," she says, and wipes her mouth. "You have that look about you, that old-soul look. That my-heart-is-too-big-for-my-own-good quality that I like in people."

"Wow," Maggie says. "I can only imagine what would have happened if I made that a full shot."

Maggie smiles, for what feels like the first time all day. This is going to be okay, she thinks, all of it. She'll go home and sleep off some of the absinthe. She'll get ready for the party tonight. And this time tomorrow, they will be on their way back to Red Hook.

Then Georgia starts to speak again.

"I just had a feeling as soon as I saw you get off the bus. I had a positive feeling, which is a relief. And I was worried about it. I had all these conversations set up in case it got awkward. Like, Nate told me you loved music. We could talk about that. Because the first time Nate was married, it didn't work like that. All the prepped conversations in the world wouldn't have helped. I tried to be nice, I wanted that, but she made it so hard. She made it really hard."

For a second, Maggie is certain she misheard her. Until she is certain she hasn't.

"Ryan never even tried with me. She wasn't the type. She's

the other type. You know, the girl you hate because you kind of want to be her? Cold, but occasionally sweet in the way that keeps men running back because they are thinking she'll be sweet again. One day. If they figure out the special way she needs them to do everything just right."

Maggie's head is spinning. It may spin right off of her body. She holds on to the side of the rock, literally holds it, trying to concentrate on her breathing, not turning toward Georgia.

"Ryan?" she says, finally.

"Right, Ryan."

"Ryan?"

"Weird name for a girl, isn't it? And she lives up to it, believe me," Georgia says, and shakes her head, in imagined shared contempt, and then—as though she is seeing for the first time that Maggie has no idea what she is talking about—she shakes her head slower, until she is barely moving it at all. "Wait, why exactly are you looking at me like that?"

Maggie doesn't answer.

"He didn't tell you he was married . . . I can't believe this. He didn't tell you about Ryan?"

"You really need to stop saying her name," Maggie says.

"How could he not have told you?" She holds her head in her hands. "This is bad. This is very bad. He's going to kill me. . . ."

Maggie isn't listening anymore. She is already standing up, starting to move back to the car. But she slips on the rock, slips and cuts open the side of her ankle, and barely catches it. The bottle of absinthe. But she does catch it, and keeps going.

"Hold on!" Georgia is jumping off the rocks, following her. "Where are you going?"

He was married. Nate was married. To a woman Maggie has never even heard of. Never even knew until this very moment.

There is no rationalizing this away. There is no excusing why he hasn't told her this.

"I don't know." She is walking in the opposite direction from the car. She is just walking.

"You need to slow down, Maggie. You need to slow down so that I can explain a little better."

She can't slow down. There are tears welling in her eyes. She can feel them. And her ankle is stinging. Now that she is standing there is no ignoring that either. The absinthe is making her head foggy, and clearer, and foggy in a whole new way. She isn't sure if she knows less than she would know otherwise, or more. It makes her think it is probably less. It makes her think she is about to make a less than great decision.

"Was Nate married?" Maggie asks.

"Yes."

"So what is there to explain?"

And this time she does start walking to the car, the keys already out, already ready to go.

"Please, wait." They are by the car again, Maggie pulling helplessly on the locked doors. Then she starts to unlock the driver's side, barely fitting the key in the lock. When she feels Georgia sneak up behind her, a quick motion, and grab the keys away.

"Maggie, you're drunk."

"I'm not drunk."

"You're not sober."

Maggie gives her a look, and Georgia holds out the keys. Then, just as she is about to grab for them, Georgia pulls them back.

"What are you going to do? You have to tell me. Are you just going to drive out of town? I can't let you do that. You can't just drive away and leave my brother. And me. Forget my brother. You can't just leave a pregnant girl by the lighthouse."

"You have a point."

"I think so."

Maggie looks back and forth between Georgia and the car. "Well then, if you want to come with me, you'll have to take me to her."

"Who her?"

Maggie doesn't say anything, just holds Georgia's eyes.

"Ryan?" Georgia looks at her like she is crazy, and maybe she is. Maybe post-absinthe, and post–too-much-information, she really is. But that is where she is going.

"What makes you sure she is near here?" she says.

She wasn't sure. But it would make sense, right? Another reason Nate dreaded coming home. The real reason. And seeing Georgia's fearful look now, she knows it. Ryan is close enough that they can get to her.

"Fine," Georgia says, pushing Maggie out of the way, getting in the driver's seat herself. "For the record, though, I think this is going to end badly. Very badly."

Maggie goes around to the passenger side before Georgia— or Maggie's own better sense—can get it together, can change her mind.

"Well," she says, "I guess we're about to find out."

Gwyn

It's not that she is entirely unfamiliar with the Internet, but she never had occasion to learn about it in too much detail, to use it too regularly. So when she found out for certain about Thomas and Eve, it was Gwyn's sister Jillian who did a Google search on Eve and sent Gwyn the results. (Who wants those kinds of results?) It isn't a good thing to have too much information. No one probably thinks of that today, but Gwyn still thinks you are better off with less information. Especially because once you start to look for it, it is because you hope you won't find it.

And then you do.

The Google search of Eve Stone revealed things that served only to make her more human, more real. Eve Stone. Full name: Natalie Eve Stone. Graduated from Pacific Valley High School in 1997. (No record of college.) Moved to Santa Barbara, California, where she lived on a street called Foothill Road, worked for a catering company, a dog-walking service, a restaurant called Firestone's. She had another address, after that, in Oxnard—under Natalie Eve Stone—maybe there was a man she lived with there, a man who supported her, because there was no record of employment. No record of employment anywhere, again, until she landed on the east end of Long Island and opened Eve's Kitchen.

It seems like she's gone by Eve for a while now, maybe more than awhile now. Gwyn doesn't know what made her decide to change it. The Internet didn't tell her anything about that.

Or this: she was Thomas's student. Eve was Thomas's continuing education student—third on the wait list, the last one he let into the class. If Stephanie Golding hadn't dropped out after the first class, Gwyn wouldn't have this problem. She'd have other problems, certainly, but not this one. And the thing is, if it wasn't actually happening to her, this problem could be out of a bad movie of the week. Where a man is supposed to be one thing. Like: bad. So they have the bad man screwing around with his student, just so the viewing audience can be clear. *Hate this guy. He's the jerk.* Like it is ever that simple, for the people who actually have the job of hating him.

These things came back to her: The night after she went to the meditation center and she found her husband not present, she decided she needed to figure out the truth. She went back through it in her mind, when it all began, that first conversation with Thomas in the bathroom, which took place right after Thomas's class on a Monday night. So the next Monday night she went to the college herself and saw Thomas and Eve outside of the library.

From the back, they didn't look so ridiculous. From the back, she could see how he fooled himself that they belonged.

He was helping her load boxes into her van, his hand hovering right above her ass, reaching for her. Like he was the one with something to prove, like he was the one who was going to have to earn her. Like if he wasn't the one reaching, Eve could just as easily move away from him.

He wanted to be the one reaching. Gwyn knew this, and it helped her figure out the rest of it—what her husband sees in Eve: Thomas is impressed by women who seem fearless, like they can do anything separate from him, like only if he is equally fearless, and lucky, and on task, is he going to be permitted to stay. If he was questioned about what he saw in her, Thomas would probably say that Eve is very sweet and unpretentious, easy to talk to. But he would be wrong to think his desire for her stemmed from any of that. Even though he appreciates those qualities, it is only in a distant way. They don't penetrate for him.

A long time ago, he had to work for Gwyn. He worked to convince her that he could be who she needed him to be: that he could stand by her and be a good parent with her and build a home life with her. Now, he wants the opposite. To earn Eve— Eve with her whimsical spirit, her desire to remain unburdened, her desire to remain plucky, daring—Thomas has to convince her that he can be as free as she is. He has to convince himself.

"We have a problem," Eve says now, still sitting on the steps.

Gwyn pretends not to hear her—or, rather, doesn't acknowledge that she has heard her—choosing instead to take the heavy tray off Eve's lap and move past her into the Buckleys' kitchen, wind blowing behind her, letting Eve be the one who follows. This time.

"Now," Gwyn says, once they are both inside, "it's looking like we may be running into a little rain, but we'll just deal with that if it happens. We already have someone who will be providing all of the alcohol, loads of champagne and caviar. A complete vodka bar. I'll have him outfit a proper waitstaff for you, so your only responsibility will be to prepare the food and have one or two staff members with you to help in the kitchen." She pauses. "You know all of this. We went over it, didn't we? Why are you looking at me like that?"

Eve looks down, away. She seems young, beneath her skin, young and scared, standing before Gwyn. It makes Gwyn feel bad for her, for a second, maternal almost. This is a young woman who is in over her head. Who has daddy issues or insecurity issues, and finds a man who promises her things. So what if that man is married? So what if he is currently breaking his most important promise to someone else?

"Ms. Lancaster . . ."

"Gwyn. Please. Considering everything."

"What's everything?"

She puts the tray on the counter. "You know," she says. "How closely we are going to be working together today."

"Well, that's what I want to talk to you about."

Gwyn turns away from the counter, and tries to look casual, pushing her hair behind her ears. "Okay."

"I am really sorry, but it turns out that I won't be able to cater the party tonight. I know this is unprofessional, so last minute, but something came up. A personal issue."

"What kind?"

"I'd rather not say."

"Except you're going to have to. You're going to have to do a little better than that, Eve. I have a hundred and seventy people showing up here in a few hours."

"I thought you said two hundred."

Gwyn crosses her arms over her chest. "I like to overorder."

Eve ignores her, motioning toward the tray. "I've already done most of the preparation, so the food belongs to you. And my friend Lola Cunningham, over at Bobby Van's, says she

will be glad to work with what I have and take over the catering duties."

Eve hangs her head, and Gwyn can see her searching for the
words—but she isn't sure which ones.

"Eve, if you are worried that this is out of your league, if that
is what this is about, please don't be. I am well aware of your
limitations, or your inexperience with a party this size, but you
have come to me highly recommended."

"By who?"

"My husband."

Eve is silent, clearly confused, wondering what Gwyn knows,
which makes Gwyn wonder how Eve figured out who she was.
"Why did you tell me that the party was here, at the Buckleys'?"
Gwyn asks.

"What are you talking about? I told you we were prepping
over here."

"No, when we spoke on the phone, what you told me was
that this was where the party was."

"You must be remembering incorrectly."

"I'm not."

Gwyn meets Eve's angry eyes. "Well, what's the difference anyway, Eve? Here or there. Here is easier in terms of space to organize. And what does this have to do with why you are canceling?"

"I guess it doesn't."

Gwyn puts the tray on the table, turns to face her. "Right, it
doesn't. So let's get started on the menu order. Obviously, you'll
be rotating among the different appetizers, but I was hoping we
could start crabcake heavy. I think those will go off well. Everyone out here is already dreading the end of seafood season—"

"Gwyn, let me be clear." She clears her throat. "I feel uncomfortable catering this party tonight."

Gwyn clears her throat, back, almost in mimicry, and moves closer to her. "So, let me be clear, you feel comfortable sleeping with my husband and helping him walk out on a thirty-five-year marriage, but you can't cater my party?"

Eve is silent, and Gwyn can see it—Eve's worst fears getting confirmed. This isn't just a bizarre coincidence, the universe delivering a karmic blow: Gwyn knows. Or, at least, Gwyn knows enough of everything that this isn't going to end well.

Eve drills her with a look. "So you do know?" she says, and she looks defiant, suddenly, and annoyed even, like she is the one who has been tricked. Like she is the one who has been wronged. And maybe, in this moment, that is the truth.

"Of course I know, Eve," Gwyn says. "Why do you think you're here?"

Eve looks beside herself, and Gwyn can see her looking at the door longingly as if wondering whether she can make a run for it. Gwyn steps in front of it to block the way. That way, at least.

"This is crazy," she says. "*You're* crazy."

"It's possible, and probably good news for you if it's true."

"Why?"

"Because that will make it easier one day when you feel bad about all of this, when you are a little more sure of yourself, when you would never dream of getting involved in someone's marriage. It will make you feel better about what you've done. Or that's giving you too much credit. What you've helped do."

"Whatever issues you have, you should take them up with Thomas. He's the one you should be talking to."

"Believe me, I will. But you still need to stay for a minute and hear me out. I still need that from you. Can you do that for me?"

Eve doesn't answer her, but she does move away from the door, goes and sits at the table and so Gwyn goes back to the counter, and starts to unwrap the tray of mushroom caps. There must be tons of other trays in the van to get to, but they will get there.

"Thank you, Eve," Gwyn says.

"You're welcome."

Gwyn finishes taking the layer of film off the container. "My goodness, these smell great!" She leans in closer. "Did you use dill? That's such an interesting choice."

"Yes, a marinade of dill and pineapple."

"Pineapple too?" She shakes her head. "I wouldn't have guessed."

"It's my mother's recipe."

"Sara Stone. Old Coast Road. Big Sur, California."

Eve gives her a look, but Gwyn just ignores it and looks back at her—into her eyes, which are bright blue, and sad. This close up, there is no denying it.

"Eve, this is not about blame, okay? Or at least this is not about blaming you. It is my husband who has betrayed me. He is the one who decided to break up our marriage. I'm clear on that. You didn't promise to stand by me thirty-five years ago. And you aren't the one who should be held responsible for what he has caused here. Or . . . not mostly."

"Then I don't understand."

"There are many reasons that I need you to cover this party tonight. Believe it or not, it's not only for my benefit."

"So it's for my benefit?"

"Partially."

"How do you figure that?"

"You don't strike me as a saver. And when my husband leaves

you, which he will, you are going to be distraught. You are going to want to get far away from here, and him, and anything that has to do with this time in your life. Maybe you'll want to go back to Big Sur. Who knows? The money you are making tonight will make it possible for you to leave."

Eve shakes her head. "This is too weird."

"Many things are, yes."

Eve folds her arms across her chest—thinking about it, really thinking about it. "In all fairness, I have to say that I think Thomas is going to choose to continue honoring our love."

"Of course you think that. Why wouldn't you? My husband thinks that. He is so certain about it, in fact, that he is willing to lie to his entire family in order to guarantee it."

Eve doesn't look confused by this, which suggests to Gwyn that he has told her what he is doing: blaming it on something that isn't blameworthy. A conversion, a spiritual change. And later, once the wounds have healed, once enough time has passed, and it is more allowed, he will have Eve meet his children, even Gwyn herself. When Eve can be aboveboard, not someone worthy of scorn. *This is my new girlfriend,* he will say. *This is Eve Stone.*

"But here's the flip side," Gwyn says. "When you love someone, when you have spent several decades loving him, you begin to see his insides even before he can see them. You know what he is going to do before he does."

"And what is he going to do? Stay with you?"

"I'm not saying that."

"What are you saying?"

Gwyn pulls the check out of her pocket, a check for twenty thousand dollars—six thousand more than they'd agreed on for tonight, just in case the extra money is helpful, just in case it came to this.

She walks up to the table, holds the check between them. "I'm saying that I think that you should take this," she says.

Eve is quiet, shaking her head. She doesn't want to take it. Gwyn understands that. To take it means to accept that things may end badly. It means to accept something that you can't consider when you are in the throes of loving someone. That he may leave, just like he left someone else. That you may not prove to be different. That you may prove to be worthy of leaving too.

"But why?" Eve says.

"Why what?"

"Why is this what you want?"

Gwyn decides to be honest for the first time that day, decides there is no harm now. She sits down across from her.

"It's not what I want, Eve," Gwyn says. "None of this. It's just what I'm doing now."

"Because you wanted to meet me? Well, you've met me."

"No, it's not for that. It's for something else."

They look at each other, and Gwyn remembers sitting here with the Buckleys so many times: when Nate was a little boy, when Georgia was just born. The time she and Thomas were sitting in these exact spots one night when Marsha made them this terrible cheese fondue, laughing together about how awful it was.

How does it happen? How does someone who was there with you, in all of those moments, let himself get so far away that he ends up putting you here in a moment like this one?

She holds out the check again. "If he loves you the way you think he does, if you're right, nothing that does or doesn't happen at this party is going to put that at risk," she says.

Eve stares at the check. And then she straightens out her jacket, her jeans. And Gwyn can see her trying to decide how badly this is going to go, trying to wager that against the large sum of money.

"You don't even have to come into the party, except to bring in the cake. And that's only because I made it. The rest of the time, the servers will take care of everything. You probably won't even see him all night."

She is silent. "I need to understand why," she says.

Because, Gwyn wants to say, *maybe I'll be able to organize it so he sees you at just the moment that I need him to.*

"I know you don't owe me anything, but you also don't *not* owe me anything. This was my family. This was my entire life. And it's not your fault. But then again, that is just semantics. Because if you didn't exist, I wouldn't be standing here. If you didn't want to be with him, all of this would be beside the point."

"He might have done this for someone else."

"But he didn't, did he? He did it for you. We are here now because he chose to do this. For you."

Eve looks at her, and for a second Gwyn doesn't know what she is going to do. That's the way it is, isn't it? And then she does it.

She takes the check out of Gwyn's hand. "Where would you like the trays?" she asks.

"The trays?"

"Where would you like me to start setting up?"

"Over there is fine," Gwyn says, pointing at the counter. "Over there would be great."

Maggie

They have driven all the way down to Amagansett—back past River Ranch Road and through Montauk town center, through the dunes off the highway, gated entrances leading to small, one-wine vineyards: WALKING TOURS AVAILABLE, Georgia going seventy, eighty miles per hour until they approach a restaurant and she hits the brakes, makes a sharp right into the circular driveway. It is a lovely restaurant in a white clapboard house—a rectangular white and black sign the only thing to distinguish it from the other houses around it, to let people know that it is a restaurant as opposed to a residence:

The House.

Rest. Bar.
Est. 1993

Maggie is quiet, looking back and forth between the sign and the restaurant. She is afraid to ask the first question that she knows the answer to.

Before she hears the answer out loud, she can still pretend there is another explanation: that Georgia is hungry and wants to get something to eat, or that she just wants to use the bathroom, and this is the first public place to stop. It is a nice bathroom—Maggie can guess, even from just peeking through the front door into the mahogany bar, candlelit, a fire already going.

"Tell me you have to pee," Maggie says.

"I do."

"Oh, thank God. For a second, I thought you were going to say this is Ryan's restaurant."

"This is Ryan's restaurant."

Maggie's chest drops. It is her fear—it is the possibility that she feared most confirmed. "Ryan's a chef?"

Georgia nods. "Ryan's a chef."

Why does this feel like the worst news there could be, the most threatening? Maggie isn't sure yet, but she knows it will come to her and that will be worse. Maggie's eyes focus back on the sign. The date of 1993, shining out at her. Nate told her that he lived here for a few years after high school. She had asked him why, and he had said something about not being ready to leave yet. Not being ready to leave yet: since when is that shorthand for *because instead of going directly to college I got married and opened a restaurant with my first wife, the one who came before you?*

"And Nate opened this place with her? This is his place too?"

Georgia runs her fingers along the steering wheel, the dashboard clock.

"Georgia?"

"You know, you're pretty good at figuring this all out. Maybe there is no need to go inside and talk to her."

"There's a need," she says, wondering how old Ryan had been when this place opened. If she was opening a restaurant already, she had to be older than Nate, probably significantly older. It reminds her of a conversation she had with Nate early on, an innocent conversation, when she asked him how he decided to be a chef, and a look came over his face. An awful look that he immediately tried to hide with a story that didn't ring true— something about watching his mother cook for the family when he was little—and a feeling Maggie tried to push down that he wasn't being honest. That *she* was being crazy, oversensitive. Because what reason would he possibly have had for not telling the truth about that? Here was her answer.

"I am going to have to call Nate when you go inside," Georgia says. "Just to tell him we're here. I'm sorry, but I don't know what else to do. I don't know how to fix this, and maybe he will."

Maggie thinks about that—about all the ways she lets Nate fix everything, about all the ways she has believed that he can. "Be my guest," she says. "The last thing we need is another secret."

She looks down and realizes that her hand is on the door handle. She realizes that she is frozen there. She doesn't open the door because when she does, she will start to have the answers to all of her questions, and maybe the only one that matters: did he not tell Maggie because it mattered so little to him or so much?

"It's not his anymore. I don't think she officially bought him out, but he has no association with the place. It's not like he's sneaking back here to cook with her or whatever."

"Now that's a relief," Maggie says.

Maggie gets out of the car and gives Georgia a smile. Then she walks up to the restaurant's front door, steps inside, before she can think about it.

It is closed still—most of the house lights off. Plants are everywhere and a smell that Maggie can't exactly make out, woodsy, like dried cherries, or pine trees, or a weird combination of the two.

Maggie takes the whole place in, and feels relief that it doesn't look like their restaurant in Red Hook. Nate hasn't tried to re-create exactly what he has left behind. That has to be a good thing, she thinks. Only then she can't help but notice that The House looks—a little disturbingly—like the exact opposite of the restaurant in Red Hook. It is full of things Nate was adamant that he didn't want for their restaurant: the brick wall and the fireplace, a granite bar, the dark walls. *Is that just as bad?*

"Can I help you?

She looks up to see a woman behind the bar, wiping down a Scotch glass. The woman is wearing a bandanna on her head and a blue tank top, her arms covered with tattoos. Beautiful dolphins and birds, clouds in the background. Thin, thin arms. Flat stomach. She looks both strong and frail, as she leans on her elbows, as though she were used to it—never moving toward anyone, letting them come to her.

"We're not open until six," she says.

"Oh, I'm not here to eat."

"Then we're definitely not open," she says.

And she smiles when she says it, but it is more of a half smirk, and Maggie takes in the rest of her face: the olive skin and eyes, pouty lips, all of which stop Maggie for a second and make her take a longer look, as if it is her job to catch it. Whatever she thinks she is missing.

"I know you're setting up, but I was just hoping to speak with Ryan . . ." She realizes she doesn't know her last name—Ryan's last name—which is when she realizes it could be Huntington. Whoever this Ryan is, her last name could be Huntington. She could still share that with Nate, too. Maggie catches the menu out of the corner of her eye. On the bottom it says *Executive Chef.* And, blessedly, it says that her name isn't Huntington. It's Engle. Ryan Engle.

"Engle," she says. "I'm looking for Ryan Engle."

The woman puts the glass down, takes out another one, and pours two glasses of Hendrick's gin. "Are you here to ask her for a donation or help with a charity drive?"

"No."

"Are you a Jehovah's Witness asking for money?"

"Not the last time I checked."

"Do you know my mother? Because she is definitely looking for money."

"None of the above."

She hands Maggie one of the glasses. *Why is everyone trying to get me drunk today?*

"Then I'm Ryan."

"I'm Maggie."

"Maggie, everyone who walks through the front door between lunch and dinner gets a shot of gin to make the rest of the day better. That's the rule."

"Really?"

"No, but I'm having a pretty crappy day, and I have this self-imposed rule about not drinking alone. Especially gin, which is my weak spot. So you're going to have to do."

"Thanks."

She tilts her glass in Maggie's direction and opens her throat, swallows it down, fast.

This is Ryan. Drinking gin. With me. I'm drinking gin with her. Ryan with the lovely arms, the pretty tattoos. Nate has seen all of them. Where are the others? There must be others. Nate would know those too. He would know everything.

"So you're Ryan?" Maggie says.

Ryan puts her glass back on the counter. "Didn't we just do this?"

"If we could just do it one more time . . ."

Ryan motions to her to have her drink, which she does, closing her eyes against it. Then Ryan pours herself another. "So why are you here again?"

What on earth was she going to say? *I have some questions about my future husband, whom you happened to be married to? I'd like you to explain what happened between you, since apparently he is unable to tell me anything that resembles the truth.*

"Wait, did you say your name was . . . Maggie?" Ryan asks.

Maggie nods. "I did."

"Oh, *Maggie,* I told you I was having a bad day!" she says, but she smiles, a real smile, when she says it. And Maggie can see it, can feel it: how intoxicating it can be to get this woman's approval.

"I'm lost," Maggie says.

"You're early. I don't need you for another hour. Did Lev tell you to get here this early?" She looks down at her watch, turns it over. "I thought Lev said that your name was Molly. I'm terrible with names, so it is probably my fault. Man, I appreciate you covering for Lev tonight. I know she feels bad about being sick again. But when you're pregnant, food is complicated. We all know what that's like, right?"

Maggie feels her eyes open wide. "Have you been pregnant?"

"Excuse me?"

Ryan shoots her a confused look, and Maggie tries to figure out a way to cover. Before she even has to, Ryan starts walking to the kitchen, assuming that Maggie will follow her, which she does.

"So the rest of the staff will get here at about four-thirty P.M., but as long as you're around we can get started prepping the first course. We only have the eight o'clock seating tonight, so I'm trying a new fig reduction on the duck. Did Lev forward you tonight's menu?"

"Probably, but my e-mail is down," she says. "So maybe you can fill me in as we go."

It is scaring her. It is scaring her how easy she is finding it to lie.

Ryan swings open the glass door to the kitchen where the food for that night is lined up on the countertop. Fresh parsley leaves and smoked mozzarella, loose peppermint and loaves of grain bread.

She hands Maggie a bowl of fresh tomatoes, all business. "We're making a spaghetti squash salad, so I'll need these boiled for about a minute, seeded, and cut up with some olive oil and fresh basil for the dressing."

She lost her at boiled.

"Easy enough . . ." Maggie says, and goes to the stovetop, takes out a small pot and gets ready to fill it with water.

Meanwhile, Ryan is standing at the countertop pulling on some figs, or doing something to them that Maggie doesn't understand. "So," she says, looking up at her. "How long have you been at the Maidstone?"

"The Maidstone?"

And Maggie realizes this must be the restaurant where the other person works. The actual person who is supposed to be helping. Maggie can't swallow. This isn't a game. This is a person standing before her. A person who was married to Nate. How incredibly insane that she is here talking to her. And yet she can't imagine getting herself to leave. At least not yet.

"Six months?" she says, like a question. And she tries to change the subject, move it closer to a subject that will lead them toward it, the reason she is here. "Did I notice on the sign outside that you've been in business since the early nineties? That's quite an accomplishment. It must have been hard to get the money together, especially starting out so young." She clears her throat. "How did you do it?"

"I had a partner at first. His family had plenty of money. And they helped us out *a lot*." She looks up at Maggie. "Too much, really. Could you hand me the olive oil?"

Maggie hands the bottle over, trying to busy her hands, trying to at least make them look busy. Her heart is threatening to beat out of her chest. *She had a partner. His family helped a lot.* Helped as in paid for the whole thing?

That would explain why, now, Nate doesn't want to take a penny from them. For the restaurant. It would explain something about being worried about making the same mistake.

"Who was he?" she asks. "Your partner?"

Ryan looks up at her, meets her eyes with something like a warning. "You ask a lot of questions, don't you?" she says.

"I'm sorry. I'm nosy sometimes. Particularly now. I do that. I didn't . . ." She looks at Ryan, and almost tells the truth, tells something—at least—a little like it. "I am in the process of deciding whether to open a restaurant with my husband, and it just seems like it could cause so many complications."

"It definitely can."

"Did it for you? I mean, was your partner your husband?"

Ryan nods. "Yes."

Maggie can't swallow.

"But, you know, this time around, it hasn't been complicated," she says. "So I guess it depends on the two people."

"So you're remarried?"

"Lev didn't tell you? She always tells me we have the best relationship she's seen, but I guess she wouldn't pass that on to you . . ."

She shakes her head. What would Lev have told her? Apparently that Ryan is very happily married. Is she married to someone who came shortly after Nate? She feels herself about to cry, cry because she is here, and because she has no idea what she is trying to find out from being here.

"Wow. I'm an asshole. You look so upset. God, I'm sorry. Don't tell Lev. Lev told me not to make you cry." She shakes her head. "I didn't even think I did anything yet. I think I'm missing the gentle gene or something."

"You didn't do anything," Maggie says.

"So what's wrong?"

"I'm not telling the truth," she says.

"Excuse me?"

"You were married to Nate Huntington, right? He was your husband at some point . . ."

She stares at Maggie with a look that could go right through her, but doesn't answer. And for a blessed second, she can still say no. Until she doesn't.

"Yes. I was married to Nate."

Maggie nods. "I know his sister pretty well. Georgia? And I just remembered that I knew already. I remembered something she had said once, offhandedly. Anyway . . . I realized that I knew that. I realized I already had the answer to my own question. You were married to Nate. And now you're not. And I apparently like the sound of my own voice . . ."

Ryan nods, looking back down at the food in front of her, going back to work. "How is Georgia?"

"Pregnant."

She smiles. "Good for her. Congratulate her for me. Not that she'll want to hear it, necessarily. But . . . and how's Nate doing? Do you know?"

Maybe, maybe not. What is the right answer?

Maggie picks up some more tomatoes. What she is doing with them is unclear to anyone. "He's doing well. He's opening a restaurant in Brooklyn, actually. In this area called Red Hook near the pier."

"I thought I heard something about that. That's great for him. That's a great thing . . . I didn't exactly handle things well with him, but you live and learn I guess, right? That's the problem. Sometimes you do it at someone's expense."

And this is her chance. Ryan will tell her now whatever it is she came here to find out—exactly what happened between them. Only why does she want to find that out? So she can know why Nate's past fell apart? It feels more merciful than that, this mission, even in its chaos. It feels to Maggie like she wants Ryan to say something—the one thing—that will make Maggie understand not why Nate's past fell apart, but why Nate has kept it hidden. What she can do so he doesn't want to hide anything else.

Only looking at Ryan—who in the twenty minutes since Maggie met her has seemed like an array of contradictions: tough and kind, sweet and biting—she wonders if maybe Nate doesn't understand himself what happened. Maybe he doesn't understand what happened, and because of that, he couldn't imagine a way to explain it to someone else.

But then the opportunity to ask Ryan anything, to test out any theory, is gone. The kitchen door swings open. And a woman in overalls walks in. A woman in overalls with brown hair, wide cheeks, and a friendly smile. One of the friendliest smiles Maggie has ever seen. And she is carrying produce. She is carrying a huge basket of fresh corn, needing to be shucked, beautiful broccoli, beets, radishes and cucumbers.

"Hey there, darling," she says to Ryan. "Sorry it took me so freaking long to get here."

"You should be," Ryan says.

Then she leans in, this woman does, and kisses Ryan on the lips, long and full. The basket of produce still in her hands, Ryan's hand reaching around to hold the back of her head.

Which is when Maggie drops it, the tomato in her hand, and it splatters on the floor. Splatters right in front of her.

"Gosh, I'm sorry," she says, and leans down to pick it up, sopping up the juice with her apron.

"Who is this?" the woman says, looking down at her.

"This is Maggie. Maggie, this is Alisa Barrett. My partner."

Here in the restaurant, here in life? But Maggie knows the answer. This is the person whom Ryan left Nate for. Maggie knows it. Does it make it harder or easier that it is a woman as opposed to a man? Probably both harder and easier. And, in the end, it comes down to the same thing, anyway: this is the person whom Ryan is with now, the person she has chosen. This is the person who, unlike Maggie, knew of the first marriage—

knew about Ryan's past—and therefore got to keep it as the past. Because she was given the chance to understand it. Because it wasn't kept secret, and given the power that a secret gets when it finally emerges. Stinging us with its history, with its preserved weight.

"Maggie is covering for Lev tonight," Ryan says.

"Not very well," Maggie says, holding up the broken tomato as proof.

Alisa Barrett laughs. She has a nice laugh, rich and full and bold, and it makes Maggie like her. It also makes her want to get out of their kitchen immediately.

"You know," Maggie clears her throat, "I'll be right back. I'll be back in, you know, no time at all."

Ryan looks over at her. "Where are you going?"

Maggie points loosely in the direction of the front room, loosely in the direction of where she imagines is a bathroom, or a car, or somewhere else that she logically needs to be. Then she is walking quickly, so quickly—through the kitchen door, back through the restaurant—that she doesn't see her until it is too late, that she runs headfirst into a girl with cropped, bleached-blond hair on her way in.

And falls.

"Whoa! Collision time." The girl pulls Maggie up to standing. "Are you okay?"

Maggie nods. "I'm sorry."

"Don't be. I shouldn't have snuck up on you. Are you Ryan?"

"No. I am definitely not Ryan." She pauses, looks at the girl, who is looking back at her confused, holding an apron in her hands—an apron she brought from somewhere else, the word *Maid* vaguely visible. "You're the one covering for Lev tonight?"

"I'm Molly Barton." She smiles, and holds out her hand.

She unties her apron, and hands it to her, starts to walk away. "It's nice to meet you, Molly," she says.

"Thanks, wait . . ." Molly calls after her. "Are you coming back?"

"Not if I can help it," she says.

And she doesn't turn around. She is going to walk out this door, and say good-bye to Georgia and find a bus stop. She is going to go anywhere but here. Only when she steps back outside, she sees him standing there, his arms crossed, waiting for her, or just waiting. In a wet suit, a UVA sweat shirt thrown over it. That dark hair on top of his head.

"Nate," she says. She says it out loud, in spite of herself.

"I thought you could use a ride."

Gwyn

They are setting up.

Trucks and florists and chair-rental people and alcohol suppliers and waitstaff, piling into her driveway, onto her lawn, parking diagonally, parking straight, making a mess of everything. Some of them are already in uniform, most in T-shirts and jeans, moving tables and lanterns and vases and linens and cases of alcohol and cases of wooden candlestick holders into the center of the barn, working hard to get everything party ready against the brewing wind.

If Gwyn chose to hire a full-service caterer, one company could have handled all of this business. There would be a supervisor. And it wouldn't be so scattered, so able to fall short in one arena, so overwhelming in another. And yet that wasn't an option. Or at least, not the most important one for Gwyn to take.

So here she sits in the nook of the wraparound veranda porch, watching as too many people from Doug's Alcohol and Spirits, Island Florists, Sanford's Rentals, and Hamptons Staffing make their way across the door walk—that small space of land between the house and the barn—while trying to go over her list for the evening of everything that needs to be handled.

Their guests will start arriving around eight for an elongated cocktail hour, complete with heavy hors d'oeuvres, good vodka, too much talk about too many things that don't matter. She wishes instantly that Jillian would be among them, wishes she hadn't asked her not to come.

But why not? I want to be there, Jillian said on the phone.

Because if you're there, Gwyn said, *it's real.*

And if I'm not? Jillian asked.

Maybe it's something else.

It *could* be something else, could just be an anniversary party that Gwyn is watching come together—that Gwyn would assume she is watching come together if she didn't know the rest of the story. If she didn't know that, at 9:30, instead of toasting their future, she and Thomas would toast their past, cut their cake, and go their own ways. Marriage over, integrity intact. Like the books suggest. Good for the family unit, good for closure. And simple. Right? If only Gwyn was feeling simple, if only that still seemed possible. A simple ending. A new beginning.

She hears someone coming up behind her, and turns to see Thomas standing above her, wearing khaki shorts and no shirt, just out of the shower. His hair wet. A glass of lemonade in his hand.

"You're back?" she says.

"I'm back."

"I didn't hear you come back."

She looks up at him, reaching for the lemonade. He hands it to her, and sits down next to her, and they watch together. She isn't particularly in the mood to talk to him, or be with him, even, but she doesn't want him to go over toward the Buckleys' place. Not that he would. Why would he? But still. It would be bad for him to go anywhere near the house and find Eve's van in the garage, Eve working inside. There is something exhilarating, though, at the possibility he might. There is something exhilarating to Gwyn in that for once she is standing between the two of them, she is the one in control.

She takes a long sip of the lemonade, the cool drink reminding her how thirsty she is, the last of the pot just now leaving her body. "Where's Nate?" she asks. "Inside somewhere?"

Thomas shakes his head, putting his hands on his knees. "I'm not sure. The phone rang. And he ran to get it. I think it was Georgia. He went out front to talk to her, and I couldn't make out what he was saying."

"She probably wants him to go meet her and Maggie, wherever they are. That's fine. The fewer people around here while everyone is setting up, the better."

Thomas turns and looks at the woodwork in the nook, running his hand along the fractures. "This needs fixing still. I'm sorry I haven't done it. I meant to do it before I left for California. You wrote me that note asking me to, didn't you? I'll get around to it, now, in the next day or two. . . ."

Would he really, though? They've discussed this already. They've discussed his taking care of this for months and months. Is he going to get to it now? Right before he leaves here, and her? Why now? It exhausts her to consider it, what she is starting to understand. That, in fact, this may be the time when someone is most able to fix something. Right at the moment it counts least.

"So did you speak to the caterer?" he asks.

"What?" She looks at Thomas, and sees that his question is innocent. Or seemingly innocent. He isn't particularly interested in her answer. "Why?"

"It's just that you were worried this morning, weren't you? And I haven't seen anyone milling around the kitchen. I've seen every other truck in the world, but none that has caterer written on it."

Gwyn smiles. "No, it's fine. Since the rest of the staff is setting up here, I asked her to go next door to the Buckleys'. I thought she'd have more space that way. To finish with preparations."

"So it's a split-level operation," he says.

"Kind of. You could say."

He nods, interested. "Why did you do it that way? Doesn't it make more work for you?"

"It made sense at the time."

"And now?"

"And now it's made more work for me."

She meets his eyes, really meets them, which is her mistake. Because he smiles, and the rest of it disappears. For a minute, it disappears. The anger, the confusion. It is someone else who caused all of this. Not this guy next to her. He is just her husband sitting on her porch with her, drinking afternoon lemonade, and waiting to see what the rest of the day will bring to them.

"Thomas," she says, and clears her throat. "You should know something. You should know this."

"Okay." He waits.

And she starts to tell him what she has been planning for tonight. But then one of the bartenders—a petite brunette in a black cap—walks by, and Thomas looks at her. He looks at her like he is trying to decide if she is pretty beneath that cap. It is a subtle look, and beside the point. This girl with her black cap isn't the problem. And the only reason that Gwyn notices is that she is looking too, wondering too. Still, the spell is broken, and Gwyn changes her mind. She changes her mind about changing anything.

Anyone who says it doesn't all come down to one moment is lying. This is it. It comes down to this for them. If she told him the truth—that she knew *his* truth, that she was plotting something for this evening—their lives would have moved in a different direction. A better one, a worse one? Who is she to judge? All she knows is that she sees the other life's possibility—and then, in her silence, she sees that life disappear.

"What, Gwyn?"

She leans toward her husband, running her hand through his hair. "Nothing," she says. "I just love you."

He is silent. It has been a long time since she's said that to him, and something settles over Thomas's face. At first she thinks it is guilt. But then it seems to be something else beneath that, something like regret. Because these words—*I love you*—have power in their absence. Almost like sex: you forget its power when it is readily available, but when it is gone for a while, it gets a chance to make itself new, to make itself mean something all over again.

So he reaches for her. He reaches for her, like he means it, because he does mean it, and in one motion, he is pulling her deeper into the nook, where someone can see them if they are looking hard, from the north, and from a distance, but where they'd have to be looking that hard. From the right angle, at the right moment: Gwyn tight against the wall, Thomas blocking her, and blocking her in.

"I love you too," he says, real low.

Then his arms are around her back, pulling up her dress from behind, his face locked in tight to her face, eyes open, not kissing, as she rips at his shorts, pulling them all the way off of him, and leaving him vulnerable like that, open, right from the beginning, forcing him to go quickly, as though they might get caught, and they *might* get caught, by their children, their impending guests, each other.

He pushes himself into her. And the world stops. Thomas stops moving quickly, his lips finding her neck, biting, Gwyn bearing down with her lower body, hard, adding pressure. Her eyes closed. She is still holding the lemonade, tight, which she doesn't realize until she does. Which is when she drops it, the glass shattering into a thousand small pieces as she reaches for her husband's back, his shoulders, and holds on.

Maggie

Maggie walks toward him, holding her left shoulder with her right hand, as if protecting herself. From him? From what's coming? He is leaning against The House sign, his arms folded across his chest. He looks upset—more distraught, though, than angry—but even so, she realizes that he may be equally mad that she has come here as she is humiliated that she felt the need to.

"Hey," she says.

"Hey." He motions in the direction of the restaurant. "How did that work out for you?" he asks.

"Pretty good. We sat down, made some excellent mint juleps, and talked about old times. She showed me your wedding album. Very lovely." She points toward where she left Ryan. "You want to go in and say hello for a couple of minutes? I'm sure she'd be glad to see you."

"You shouldn't have come here," he says.

"No kidding," she says. She looks out behind him, the wind kicking up, the clouds covering up what was left of the sun. "Where's the car?"

"Across the street, by the dunes. I worried that you would need to make a quick getaway."

"And?"

"And I decided not to let you."

She looks at Nate, meeting his eyes, and has to bite her lip hard, to stay composed. Because now it is real. He is standing before her, and they are standing here in front of the restaurant, and she can't ever go back to not knowing the things she knows now. She can't go back to that complacent feeling she had that things were simple between them, or one way. That illusion, in all its glory, ends here.

Staring back in the direction of the restaurant, she realizes there is a more pressing issue. The real kitchen sub has probably introduced herself by now, and Ryan or Alisa, or both, will want some answers.

"You know, in about five more seconds, someone is going to come out here trying to figure out who I really am. So unless you want a less-than-happy reunion, we should probably walk."

"Okay." He nods, and points in the direction of the ocean, and they start walking that way. She doesn't know exactly where they are going, but she keeps up with him—keeps a few feet away, but keeps up with him—until they cross the road and head down the small hill, the small houses dotting it, past the green sign that says PRIVATE BEACH.

And then the Volvo is there—the one that Eve hit this morning—in a small, otherwise empty parking lot. But instead of getting in the wagon, Nate walks past it, over the rocks, toward the beach itself.

Maggie stops on the rocks, holds her ground. "I don't want to sit down on the beach, Nate. I don't want to pretend everything's okay."

He turns back to look at her, his hands shoved into his sweat-shirt's pocket. "And if we're standing here, things are less okay?"

"Yes."

He nods, but she can see him starting to crack a little, getting defensive. "So we'll stand here, if that's what you want."

"I don't want *any* of this," she says. "You were married? How is that possible? How is it possible that you didn't feel a need to mention that any time over the last eighteen months?"

"It's not that simple," Nate says.

"It's also not that complicated."

He is silent, looking away from her. This is his worst nightmare, this kind of confrontation, and it almost makes her feel bad for him. If she weren't feeling so bad for herself, she'd stop this.

"I don't know what you want me to say, Maggie."

"How about you're sorry?"

"I am sorry."

"For not telling me, or that I found out?"

"Both."

"Not good enough," she says. And suddenly she realizes nothing is going to make this good enough.

"Okay, let's start easier, *Champ*. What have you told me that's right? Because apparently I know nothing about your past. Not the type of high school you went to, or your family's situation, or your most significant relationship before me. Don't you think any of that information would have told me something about you?"

"It doesn't."

"It doesn't?"

He shakes his head. "The information that is relevant about me is that I left here, and went to school and moved to California and fell in love with you. All the rest of it is . . . prologue."

She shakes her head, thinking of the messiness of her

parents' split, of growing up on her own without a mother, of all the things she disclosed to Nate late at night, that were hard for her, hard to acknowledge as having to do with herself—the pieces of herself she'd like to be less true.

"I feel cheated," she says.

"Why?"

"All this time, and you didn't even show me yourself. These things . . . they are who you are."

"No, they are who I was."

"No, they are who you are. They brought you here. To this day. You didn't give me a chance to understand that even the unattractive parts of you, the messy parts, were something that I could accept."

"You believe that? Can you try for a second to understand that maybe my decision to leave this all behind has nothing to do with you?" His voice is tightening, as if he is failing to keep a lid on it, his own growing anger, which instead of making Maggie step back fuels hers. "It was a decision I made long before I ever met you, Maggie."

"What decision is that? To just pretend that everything is okay, even when it's not? You couldn't hear your mother tell you what was really going on with the party tonight. You couldn't hear me ask you to be real with me about your childhood here. You think if you don't talk about it, you can just pretend everything is all right? Everything is not all right. Not with us, not with your parents, not with anything today. And if you let yourself go anywhere real with it, you have to acknowledge it."

"Which part?"

"That I had a right to know. I had a right to know that the person I was marrying had been married before. I had a right to know why it didn't work out between you. For goodness' sake, doesn't that make sense? I had a right to know more about you than a stranger might."

"You do."

Do I? She doesn't know if that's true. She doesn't know what she believes. How do you ever know anyone, at the end of the day? Does it matter if they leave out who they used to be? Does it matter if they are never going to become who you thought they were?

She starts to walk away, back toward the car. She can't think about it now, she can't think until she has some distance. Until she has some time when she isn't looking at him, and letting what she feels for him obscure what she needs to be remembering right now.

"I don't think she ever loved me."

She turns back around, because she hears the anger drop out of him, hears something much worse beneath it. "Excuse me?"

"We met and it all happened so fast. We met two months before I graduated from high school, and were married six weeks after. I had never known anyone like her. That sure of herself, that fearless about everything. She always knew exactly what she wanted. She knew exactly how she felt about everything that came her way." He paused. "It is a dangerous reason to love someone."

"What is?"

"Because you want to be them."

She is quiet, looking at him. She can see in his eyes how hard it was for him to say that—to her, to himself. She knows the last thing he wants to do now is to keep going.

"And I'm sure she would say she did love me. But I can't stop thinking that she was in it because I could help her. She needed help getting the restaurant together, getting this life together that she wanted. And when she didn't need that help anymore, she didn't need me anymore. And I'm not just talking about financial support or whatever. I'm talking about the fact that she wanted an audience, and I couldn't have been a better one. I'm talking about how long it took me to believe, after her, that anyone would actually just want me."

"So what, then?" Her heart is racing, everything good he has said dropping out beneath what she fears she just figured out, what she worries she now knows. "Is that why you picked me?"

"What are you talking about?"

"I'm the opposite." She motions in the direction of The House. "Ryan, your previous life, the restaurant. It looks absolutely different, it feels absolutely different. You just said it yourself, and I saw it myself. She couldn't be more different from me . . . the way she looks, the way she is. And so now I don't know if you actually chose me, or just chose the opposite of what didn't work before."

"I am choosing you."

But she is no longer listening. She is not even sure, at this moment, that she knows how. Apparently, though, she does know how to cry. Because she is crying. She is crying harder than she can remember crying. She can't stop it now. And, what's worse, she can't stop from saying the next thing, even though she is scared it will change everything once they both hear it.

"And the worst part is that commitment has always been so hard for me. You know that. You know that I've run from everyone my entire life. But when I met you, I thought, hey, maybe it isn't me, *after all*. I just had to meet the right person. And then I'd know how to stay still, and be a good partner, and be a good friend, and be happy." She pauses, makes herself swallow. "Only now, I think that our relationship is the clearest example I can give myself that I still can't handle commitment, that some-where inside I still don't want real partnership."

"Why?"

"Because there was no real risk with you," she says. "You were going to run first."

"I'm right here."

"That's the thing, Nate. Why do I have to explain this to you? If you haven't been honest with me, you've never been here," she says.

She starts to leave him standing there, but the sound of his voice stops her. "So now you have it, Maggie. Your way out."

"You think I was looking for one?" she says.

"You think you're not going to take it?" he says.

Then he is silent, and in the silence she has no choice but to feel it, beneath the pain, beneath her sadness—a loosening in her chest, the quick release—a little something like relief. She can go now.

She looks back in the direction of the restaurant. She follows the skyline north and east toward Montauk Point, toward the bluffs and the cliffs that, through the fog, she can barely see. She follows the skyline until she can see it. The outline of the house. Her wallet is there, her belongings, the things that can get her away from this, and here.

And she starts to walk that way.

part three

the divorce party

Gwyn

If the ending makes you think of the beginning then maybe that explains why Gwyn is standing under the stream of shower water, thinking of her wedding day. September 23, 1972: no photo album to remind her, no announcement in the *New York Times*. They had forgone a big wedding, forgone any of the requisite hoopla. This was partially because Gwyn didn't care about that stuff, and partially because she thought it would bring them bad luck. To make too big of a deal out of what she felt so blessed to find.

They had only a few people at the wedding: her parents, Thomas's parents, their sisters. All of them standing on the cliff outside. Looking out over the water. She spent the morning getting ready, and then walked herself downstairs into the garden. She was wearing a yellow cotton dress that she had bought in town for $65. Thomas was in a pair of linen pants, a loose white button-down, bare feet. Her father married them, only saying God one time at the end. This was their concession to him. His concession to them: the whole thing took fifteen minutes. Then they went for a long walk by the beach, stopping on the way back at a fish shack along Old Montauk Highway to have cheeseburgers.

A wedding meal of cheeseburgers and spicy fried potatoes and Coca-Cola and chocolate chip cookies.

She steps out of the shower, beginning to dry off. And she rolls open the stained-glass window, puts her hand outside. The air is misty. It is going to rain. It is going to rain, and—based on the weird colors in the sky—probably worse than the radio guy predicted. She can still make the game-time decision to have the party inside, but she doesn't want to do that. Even if the alternative is the barn falling down. Even if it falls down all around them. Something is stopping her from moving the party inside, something she can't put her finger on. It doesn't matter anyway. She doesn't need a reason. If anyone feels the mist, gets uncomfortable, they can go home. Tonight is for her, and her alone. And she will act as if that is true. She will keep telling herself this until she believes it.

When she starts to walk back into the bedroom, she hears someone there, and thinks that it is going to be Thomas. It started a long time ago—this ritual that they have of lying down on top of the bed together, fully dressed, before going to any party, even one they are hosting. It was one of Gwyn's first signs, this past year, that she was losing Thomas, that she was really losing him for good. He would still come with her to dinner parties and weddings and other obligatory functions, but he wouldn't come into the bedroom to be with her first—wouldn't have the low-voiced pillow conversation that used to be her favorite part of any evening out. If she has to guess, he stopped liking the idea they'd always had of reminding each other that this is what they were coming home to at the end of any given night. Each other. And putting that first.

So when she hears noise in the bedroom, hears someone moving around in there, her heartbeat speeds up, involuntarily.

But it isn't Thomas. It's Georgia. It's Georgia half-balancing against the bedpost, while she unsuccessfully aims to reach around herself and zip up the back of her dress: a flowery halter-top, which is beyond stuck, her back pushing out of it.

Georgia doesn't turn around but, as she continues to try zipping, she must sense Gwyn's presence, because she starts talking.

"It fit last week, and now it's too small," she says. "*Seven lousy days.* Things shouldn't be able to change so fast."

Gwyn walks toward her daughter. "We'll make it fit," she says.

"How, Mom? How are we going to do that?"

Gwyn takes a seat on the edge of the bed, tightening her towel around herself, around her breasts, Georgia moving in front of her so she can take a clear look at the zipper—the fabric stuck inside of it.

"I just don't understand what's going on," Georgia says. "People have to get better about lying around here. Or at least telling those of us in on the truth what it is that we're not supposed to spill."

"What did your father tell you?" she says, and feels her face getting red, thinking that Georgia had come across Thomas and her on the porch.

"My father?" Georgia turns around, faces her. "I'm talking about your son. Your son and his fiancée. I'm talking about a very bad chain of events I was just a part of. He didn't tell her about Ryan. Did you know that?"

"Yes, he told me."

"Well, someone should have told me!"

Gwyn puts her hand on the small of Georgia's back, starts to fiddle with the zipper, moving it slowly at first, loosening the fabric, trying hard not to think about what her daughter may say next.

"We just went to The House."

"As in Ryan's restaurant?"

"As in Ryan's restaurant, yes. Maggie was going to go with or without me and so I figured better with me. And when we got there and she went inside, I called Nate. It was the best I could do." She pauses. "They are back now. I just heard them get back, so I ran in here. I ran in here, midzip, and now the whole situation is stuck."

Gwyn tries to imagine what the two girls said to each other, what Nate and Maggie are saying to each other now, how either part of the equation can end well. Gwyn looks up at her daughter. "He should have told her. He should have told her long before now. You really can't blame yourself. It's good that it came out. It's not your fault."

"No. It's yours."

"Mine?"

"A lot of badness is coming from today. A lot is coming out of this divorce party."

"This divorce party? How is that responsible?"

"It's putting something in the air." She starts to cry, deeply and terribly, sitting down, exhausted, on her mother's lap. "I can't reach Denis."

"That's obvious." Gwyn wraps her arms around her.

Georgia shakes her head, wiping at her eyes. "Things have been a little hard on us since he's been away, but being here is really screwing me up. It's making me wonder whether I am right that we are actually happy, or whether he is going to call any minute and say that he's staying in Nebraska to be with some asymetrically haired, secretly miserable, post-hipster music snob, who moved to Omaha because the lower east side is closing down all the good music venues to make room for blue condominiums," she says. "And that sucks, *yes,* but so does she."

"What are you talking about?"

Georgia hangs her head. "I'm not sure."

Gwyn rubs her daughter's back, and then pushes her back to standing, taking a moment to focus on the zipper. "Georgia," she says. "Listen to me for a second. You're getting ahead of yourself. If you can't reach him, maybe that means he is on a plane. Did you consider that?"

"Of course, but like you want that to be the case. Like you don't think I'd be better off without him."

"I never said that."

"You didn't have to."

Gwyn thinks about this, and doesn't want it to be true. If it is, she has failed in the number one way she was hoping to succeed: she wanted to parent differently from her parents. She wanted to only want for her children what they want for themselves, even if she doesn't agree with it, even if she wouldn't hope for that. She thinks she has been good at it most of the time, but maybe not. Not if she hasn't succeeded in convincing them that she is behind them, no matter what.

"The thing is that you think we're like you and Dad," Georgia says. "But we're not."

"What are you talking about?"

Georgia pauses. "You think I love him more."

She can't see Georgia's face, but if she could, she knows she would see those eyes blazing. Sad. And hurt. Maybe she should be offended, but all she can think is: How do you avoid getting here? How do you pull your daughter back from such a sad place? If this sadness is something she has passed on, she wants to take it back, take all of it back and bear the burden herself. Make different choices, be braver, do just about anything so her daughter thinks she is worthy of getting everything that she needs as opposed to trying to figure out how to be better at giving it away.

Gwyn pulls her wet hair back off her neck, waits a minute to speak again, waits in the hope that putting a small wedge of time in will help Georgia hear her, will help Gwyn hear herself. But she has no idea what to say. What does she know right now that is hopeful? That wouldn't scare someone, if she started to say it out loud?

"Did you know that you were conceived at a Pete Seeger concert?"

Georgia looks disgusted. "Um, no. And, more importantly, that sentence should *never* be repeated."

"How did I never tell you that?"

"I never asked."

"Well, it's true. The night started off so great. We went to see him play in upstate New York. I can't remember the name of the place, but it was somewhere near Beacon, New York, and it was this great night. Starry, beautiful. Except your father and I started to fight, about something. Something silly, and I went running back to the car crying. I think I was still so scared then that fights could end us that when he got back to the car, I kind of attacked him."

"Oh my gosh." Georgia covers her ears with her hands. "What did I do to deserve hearing this? And what is your point?"

She pulls her daughter's arms back down, going back to work again on the zipper's most stuck part. "My point," she says, "is that my parents never told me anything. Everything was always cloaked, hidden. And I always promised myself that I'd be different when it was my own family. I'd tell you guys everything. Even small things, like about the concert. Because it might tell you something about you. Like maybe that's the reason you like music so much."

"I seriously doubt it."

"Still. I guess I haven't done a good job of that. Of being open?" She turns Georgia to the side, the zipper releasing slightly. "If I had, you and Nate would be better at it, at being open yourselves . . . I think when you are back here, you go back to thinking things are supposed to look a certain way. If they look a certain way, you are safe. If they don't, you're in trouble."

"Isn't that what you think?"

Gwyn looks up at her daughter, makes her meet her eyes. "What I think is that there is no good way or bad way. And the sooner we let go of expectations about how things are supposed to go, the happier we get to be."

Georgia smiles at her, puts her hand on her head. "Wow."

"What?"

"That sounds awfully Buddhist of you, Mom."

"Please . . ." Gwyn shakes her head, looking away.

"No, seriously," Georgia says, smiling bigger now. "Dad would be impressed. You are getting wiser about this stuff than he is. Maybe we have a double conversion on our hands here. Wouldn't that be something? There would be no reason for you guys to get divorced, after all."

"All right, enough," she says. "Help me here."

And Georgia sucks all the way in—as much as her pregnant belly will allow—holding her shoulders tight against her back, her ribs as in as they can go. And Gwyn is able to do it, finally. She pulls once, and then once more, and gets the zipper all the way up.

"There we go."

Georgia pulls her dress down tighter over her legs, going to look at herself in the mirror, now that the dress is up and ready.

"Not bad?" Gwyn says.

"Not bad."

Which is when Thomas walks in.

He is in his suit, his tie undone, but already in his suit. He looks back and forth between Gwyn and Georgia. "Oh, I'm sorry," he says. "I didn't want to interrupt. I was looking for you."

He is talking to Gwyn, and she knows it, knows it by how he is being soft when he says it. He has come to take this time with her, lying down together, as if that is something they still know how to do. Except Georgia is still looking in the mirror. And neither of them wants to ask her to leave.

Thomas meets Gwyn's eyes, and points, behind himself, toward the door. "You know, I'll just see you down there," he says.

Gwyn nods from the edge of the bed, and smiles at him. "I'll see you down there," she says.

Then right before he leaves, he smiles at her, smiles at her in her towel. "You look beautiful," he mouths.

"Thank you," she mouths back.

Then she watches her husband go.

Maggie

She only brought a small bag out here, which she hasn't even unpacked yet, and so she takes it with her. Her outfit for tonight is folded on top: an ivory tank top and a knee-length green skirt, her freshwater pearl earrings in their small metal container. Nate bought them for her in Berkeley last year. The earrings. She offhandedly told him that she saw them at a store—earrings that were pretty, but too expensive—and he went back to the store in the hope of surprising her with them. Only she described them badly, or he heard the wrong things, and he came back with these earrings instead: these dangly earrings, with black opals running among the pearls. But she loves the earrings, loves them even more than the earrings she noticed herself, and not only because every time she puts them on she gets to think of his going into that store for her, trying to be good to her in a way she had trouble being for herself. But for this reason, if no other, Maggie takes the earrings out of her bag, out of their case, and leaves them on his dresser behind his orange Steelers mug, where he won't find them.

Then she takes the backstairs down. Nate is still in the shower. Why should she be sneaking out of here like a criminal?

Why should she be the one sneaking? Nate is the one who created this situation. Yet it doesn't make her feel better because,
on the other side of the blame, she is still leaving him. So what
good does the blame do her? It just reminds her that it feels like
she doesn't have a choice in anymore.

And she can barely stand to picture him getting out of the
shower, towel wrapped around his waist, expecting to find her on
the bed, where he left her. Waiting to talk. Waiting to try and get
somewhere. In her place will be a note, saying she can't do this.
Not tonight, at least. Maybe she'll feel better able to deal with
everything back in Brooklyn. Back home in Red Hook. Maybe.

Now, she just needs to go. She feels that clearly. But on the
bottom of the staircase, she stops in front of the small window
and looks outside. She can see it from here: the barn lit up and
glowing, like an oversized nightlight. White balloons and water
lilies everywhere. Bundled sticks in six-foot vases. Lemon center-
pieces. The only color, the only break.

People are already starting to arrive. They look like movie
star versions of themselves: the women in cocktail dresses, the
men in perfect tan jackets. Like there is really something to
celebrate. Everyone holding single-malt Scotch or champagne
flutes.

Maggie steps outside, closing the door quietly behind her. It
is raining, slow and heavy drops. The sky dark with the promise
of more to come. Part of her is resolved to walk down into town
anyway, but she doesn't know these roads particularly well. Can
she remember how they got here? She thinks so. Right, left,
right, right. Reverse it. She thinks she can figure it out. And,
still, the last thing Maggie wants is to get lost, and end up back
here, end up anywhere near back here. She wants to be on the
green and white bus heading back to New York, heading back to

Red Hook and her neighborhood bar, Sunny's. When everyone asks where Nate is tonight, she will say he is out at his parents'. She will drink a glass of Maker's Mark for him. She will get to pretend that this is okay.

As she heads down the driveway, she catches it out of the corner of her eye. The house next door, Victorian like Hunt Hall. But slightly smaller. The Buckleys'. The beam of the light outside the screened kitchen door shining down on someone smoking a cigarette, someone Maggie recognizes.

Eve, the caterer.

She is standing beneath the awning. The smoke rises up to meet the light above it, making her look foggy, backlit, in her low-riding braids, her red chef jacket and high-top sneakers.

As Maggie moves toward her, she can see what a mess Eve is: her jacket splotched and sweaty, her hair curling out of its tight bun. She is leaning back against the screen, and doesn't notice Maggie until she is right in front of her, her eyes opening in surprise.

"It's you," Eve says, and offers a large smile.

"It's me."

Maggie holds out her hand, which she has found can be awkward even under the best of circumstances between women, but now even more so, because Eve has to put the cigarette in her mouth, hold it there, in order to shake back.

"Sorry," Maggie says.

"No, no, don't be." Eve shrugs. Then she shrugs again for good measure. "It's good to see you."

"I'm sorry to interrupt the one break you've got."

"I'm taking far more than one," Eve says.

"What?"

"Nothing." Eve shakes her head, and pulls out the cigarettes from her pocket, opening the pack for Maggie. "Would you like?"

"Yes, but I'm not going to."

Eve nods, closing the pack back up, looking back between it and Maggie. "Well, will you take them from me anyway?" she says, holding it out. "I'll just smoke the rest of them otherwise. It's turning into one of those nights, and they are never good for anyone."

"The nights or the cigarettes?"

"Both," Eve says.

Maggie smiles and puts the cigarettes in her back pocket, looking behind Eve into the kitchen. There are several servers in there, organizing food onto trays, milling around. "You're gearing up?"

"You could say that," she says, taking a peek behind her. Then Eve looks at Maggie, and Maggie can see her take in her fraying jean skirt and white tank top, trying to make sense of it. "Shouldn't you be getting ready?"

"Yes," Maggie says.

She can't go into anything more than that. She figures that Eve will hear the rest, or she won't. Either way, that is all she's got to give for now. And Eve seems to understand what she isn't saying, nodding in response, slowly at first, then quicker. And she doesn't ask her for any more than that. Not yet.

Eve gestures back in the direction of the kitchen. "Do you want to come in?"

"No, I should go," she says. "I was actually just hoping for a flashlight?"

"A flashlight? You're walking into town or something?"

Maggie nods. "That's the plan."

"It's not a good one. It's really going to start coming down, and these hills are dangerous in the rain. You don't know what it's like when it storms around here. You can end up flooded in somewhere."

"What do you suggest?"

"Tyler can take you. Remember Tyler from the van this morning? He just went on a run to Watermill for me, but he'll be back in a few minutes, and I can have him drop you anywhere you need to go."

"I just want to get to a bus."

"Not a problem. You can hide out here until then."

"Who says I'm hiding?" Maggie says, maybe too defensively.

Eve just smiles. "Come and help me inside for a little bit. I'm in the dining room, setting up some trays of prosciutto-wrapped asparagus. You can help me assemble."

"I'm not very good at assembling."

"It's just ham and asparagus," she says. "I'm really not worried about it." She pulls open the screen door, giving Maggie room to walk through it.

"Okay then," Maggie says.

She switches her bag to her other arm as they walk into the kitchen: a twelve-foot-tall ceiling, pipes running across the top, a beautiful stainless steel oven set—as high quality as any restaurant in the country. Plants everywhere.

Nate's high school.

Awesome.

Two of Eve's waiters are tending to something on the stove, another by the console putting the finishing touches on a tray of crabcakes—and Eve doesn't say anything as they pass them, through a swinging door, and into the dining room, which reveals itself to be a strange combination of red Zen-inspired furniture and Scottish dolls behind a heavy glass case.

Eve motions to the case with her head, as she takes a seat at the long dining table, getting ready for the work at hand. "Rumor has it that the dolls are worth over two million dollars," she says.

"Each?" Maggie asks.

"Man, I hope not."

Maggie puts her bag down and stares into the glass case. Is this what Nate stared at during high school? She notices it in the reflection of the glass: a picture of Murph on the mantel. She looks young—sixteen, seventeen—surrounded by a bunch of other kids. And in the corner of the picture, there is Nate. In jeans and a Mets baseball cap. Looking almost exactly as he does now. She doesn't know if that is good news or bad news.

Maggie takes a seat catty-corner to Eve, a silver tray of the meat and vegetables between them. In a purposely exaggerated way, Eve gingerly picks up a stalk of asparagus, a small piece of the ham, and wraps them together before placing them on the serving tray.

"You think you've got that?" she says.

"You may have to show me again."

Eve laughs, and they get to it, working silently at first, Maggie checking the clock in the corner every thirty seconds, like she can hurry it along: Tyler getting here. Her leaving. Her making the bus home. But soon, she gets into it—the easy preparation repetition, helping her get mindless.

"You talk a good game over there," Eve says, after a while, pointing down at Maggie's handiwork. "But you're pretty good at that. It's nice, the way you are setting them up—"

"I wouldn't get carried away," she says.

"No, really. It all looks good. You've got a knack for it. Are you planning to help Nate with food prep during the soft opening?"

"Not unless he makes me," she says. But she bites her bottom lip thinking about it. How she had made a habit of that back in San Francisco, helping him prepare the food for the night: Nate turning on the record player to old Van Morrison, the two of them sitting silently, working together.

Then something occurs to her. "How did you know that? That we're opening a restaurant?"

Eve hesitates, reaches for more vegetables. "Oh, Gwyn must have told me." Then, as if thinking better of it, she shakes her head. "You know what? That's not true. Nate's dad told me."

"Oh, so you met Thomas?"

Eve nods. "Yes," she says. "I met Thomas."

Maggie looks back down at her pile of asparagus, thinking about Thomas: how looking at him earlier today felt like looking at her future. This morning, she thought she understood what was happening in her own future. She was in love. How can everything change in the space of a few hours? Maybe that's the only way everything changes. Just when you finally believe that anything is stable, and will stay the same.

"It's hard, isn't it?" Eve says.

"What?"

"Ending up in a situation you never thought you'd be in. Or maybe the very one that you thought you'd end up in, but were trying to avoid."

Maggie meets Eve's eyes. She wonders what Eve thinks she knows. Is there something people can discern about their relationship, just by watching her and Nate?

Eve shrugs. "Just a guess," she says.

"Based on what?"

"All shame tends to look the same."

Maggie looks at her, really looks at her, and then starts to speak. "I found out today that Nate's family has quite a bit of money he never told me about. And that's the best news I got."

"What was the worst?"

"He's been married before. He's been married before to a woman he never even bothered to mention to me. And the woman is this incredibly sexy, tough woman with perfect arms who I went to see in person, because, you know, I didn't feel bad enough already."

Eve shakes her head. "Wow. Not a good day."

"Not a great one, no."

Eve puts a piece of prosciutto down and looks at Maggie. "How did you find all this out?"

She thinks back to early this morning, how it all started, stumbling on the statements that listed Nate's name as Champ. Stumbling on what was the beginning of a very different story from the one she thought she knew about the person who mattered to her most—the person she thought she knew the most about.

"I could see that Nate was trying to tell me himself, but he couldn't seem to get there. He couldn't seem to . . . trust me."

Eve is quiet in response. She is so quiet that Maggie can't help but wonder what she is thinking about. Maybe something else entirely. Maybe her mind has drifted to her responsibilities—the party—to everything going as planned.

Then she starts to speak. "I know they must seem so huge right now," she says. "The lies he has told you. All the things he has chosen to omit. But I'm thinking it's not that simple."

"What do you mean?"

Eve shrugs. "Well, there are two ways to look at this. The first is that Nate has lied to you about everything that is of any importance to who he is and how he has grown up, and what has mattered to him. His family, his money, his marriage. His first marriage, I mean. To this other woman." She clears her throat. "But, the second option you have is to interpret it differently—"

"I'm not sure I'm following."

"As really just one lie. That it is really just one lie you're dealing with here. And Nate may have done it loudly, but it's a lie we often tell ourselves, and the people closest to us."

"Which is what?"

"I get to start over."

Maggie stares at Eve, as she wonders if Eve understands more or less than she does.

"What?" Eve says. "Why are you looking at me like that?"

"I'm just wondering if you think that makes it okay? Withholding so much?"

"I think it just means that I understand. We all want that, don't we? A chance to be new, to not be the people we wish we hadn't been. The problem is that the faster you run from something, the harder it hits you when it catches up to you again."

"Well, today definitely hit me hard," Maggie says.

Eve nods. "It probably hit Nate a lot harder."

Her pulse starts to race—to race with something like sadness, like impossible compassion. Not just for her, but for Nate. With how hard and desperately, all of a sudden, she understands he has been running. Maggie remembers when she left Asheville at seventeen, thinking she could be someone new. And maybe at different points, with new scenery and new people, she has felt new. Except, really, she is still herself. Same worries about staying present, committing, being still. Same desire to make things clean when they're not. Same need to understand things as black and white, or avoid them altogether.

"Look, I'm not trying to make you more upset here. I understand what it feels like to have things going on that you don't want to say out loud."

"Like what?"

"Like I'm in love with someone who I shouldn't be in love with. Like I've been complicit in letting him break up his family so we can give being together a real shot. Like I've encouraged him to do this."

Maggie looks at Eve, trying not to judge. During college, she was seeing her TA, who lived with his girlfriend. Maggie didn't know about the girlfriend when they started, but when she found out she didn't leave him immediately either. She told herself, at the time, that it was his responsibility to stop it, to deal with his obligations. She knows now that it isn't that simple. She believes now that it shouldn't be.

"He's leaving his wife for you?"

"He seems to be." She moves the completed tray out of the way. "And then what am I going to do with him?"

Maggie laughs, running her hands through her hair. Then, giving Eve a small smile, she looks away.

"I think maybe there is another question you can ask yourself," Eve says.

"And what's that?" she says. "Do I want to try?"

She shakes her head. "Am I sure I don't?"

Maggie is silent.

"I'm just saying that's the one that will kill you one day if you're not sure and you get the answer wrong."

Maggie isn't sure of anything—which is the main reason she

smiles at Eve, and excuses herself. "I'm pretty sure I want to go and wash up," she says. "Probably should have done that before helping with the food. Is the bathroom that way?"

"Live and learn," Eve says, raising her palms.

Then she points behind herself, and Maggie heads that way, toward the back of the house, toward the master suite, toward the bathroom. But as she opens the door, she remembers what is going to be waiting for her. The special padded bathroom, the special tub. Only the bathroom that greets her is old, and not particularly noteworthy.

And there is no padding on the bathroom tub. None that she can see. The tub is white and oval shaped and too small to hold two people at all comfortably. Maggie gets in and lies all the way back, putting her arm over her eyes, her legs hanging over the edge. She tries to take a few deep breaths in, center herself, figure out what she is going to do next.

She needs to decide whether to find out the answer to the question running through her head right now, in this moment in her life: *What happens if I stay?*

Which is when Tyler walks in.

She doesn't say anything, just takes her arm off her eyes, blinks. He looks back at her for a moment, and she imagines she is some sight: curled into the tub, in her skirt, her flip-flopped feet hanging out over the side.

"Hey there," he says.

"Hey."

"So am I taking you somewhere," he says pointing in the direction of the driveway, "or are you taking a bath?"

Gwyn

This is perhaps what a wedding is supposed to be like: the barn is gorgeous and full of people, music playing, everyone eating and laughing and swaying. Everything's candlelit and lantern-lit and dreamlike. You can hear the rain in the background, feel it tumbling along the roof but you almost don't notice it, except for the light wind it is kicking up and inside—making everyone stand a little closer together.

It all makes Gwyn feel like it is appropriate that she has chosen to wear white. A handmade corseted top, a loose silk skirt. Her hair pulled back with a lily. When she wore yellow on her wedding day, her sister asked her if she was sad that she wasn't taking her one chance to be the one in all white. *I'll have another chance,* Gwyn said. She meant at a party or an event. She didn't imagine the event would be for the end of her marriage.

No one notices her at first. She is standing just inside the barn's entrance, the rain falling down behind her, taking it all in. The party is beautiful from this angle. Everyone is drinking champagne and talking in small circles. Even in this weather, everyone has come. If she could zoom in, wire her guests with hidden microphones, she still believes they wouldn't be talking about her. Everybody gets divorced now, don't they? Half of everybody, at least. The important part, for them, is that they have a nice party to go to on a less-than-nice night.

She looks straight across the barn and sees Nate and Georgia standing by the bar: Georgia sipping Nate's beer. She decides to let them be. If the divorce party leaves them hating her a little but feeling more bonded with each other, then fine, she'll take it. If they come out of this closer—more sure that they will always have each other, that this is their primary family relationship—Gwyn will feel better. She isn't dying yet, but it is one more thing she wants in line before she does. That her children will always feel loved.

Then she notices Thomas, center-barn, wearing the suit she picked out for him, laughing with the Jordans, Daniel and Shannan, who live off of Dune Road, on the bay. They got divorced themselves, maybe ten years ago now, and Shannan moved to New York City and took up with a male ballet dancer. Now Daniel and Shannan are together again, permanently again. *I'm simply too tired to not be with Daniel,* Shannan told Gwyn when she moved back out here. *And I don't think that is the opposite of love.*

Thomas waves at her. She waves back and points up to the steel rods, then the weather outside—the lightning coming in quicker, brighter bursts; the barn starting to seem too much like a bull's-eye. But Thomas just shrugs, as if to say: *let's not worry about it.*

Fine. He doesn't want to worry, they won't worry. Let him have his way this last time. This barn will come crumbling down or it won't. Only, he won't get to tell her again that she always worries too much. She wants his last memory of her tonight to be that she didn't care, didn't overanalyze, didn't take on the role of worrier for both of them. For once, she would relax into acceptance of whatever would come. That she, for once, was willing to breathe in and let even the most rational fear go.

A waiter comes by and offers her a braised lamb chop. She takes it, because what else is she going to do? She has a small bite, and looks around at the other waiters carrying trays of spicy cashews and barbecued chicken bites, ahi tuna crackers and soybeans, Thai toast and curry tofu—all disappearing into people's palms as soon as they appear.

She notices Minister Richards with his wife and decides to go over to say hello, when she feels a pat on her back, and turns to see Maxwell Scalfia, a five-foot-tall doctor who works with Thomas, married to Nicole, another doctor, who is a good ten inches taller than he is. She used to see him almost daily, all those years when it was Thomas and her habit to have lunch together. Mondays and Wednesdays, most Fridays too.

"How are you holding up?" Maxwell asks, stepping on his toes to kiss her cheek.

"Fine, Maxwell, we're doing fine. Thank you for coming tonight. We're glad to have you."

"We're glad to be here."

She smiles, wondering how long she has to stand here—before she can move on. He will be Thomas's friend now. And as far as Gwyn is concerned, Thomas can more than have him.

Maxwell is still smiling at her, though, making eye contact, and tipping his glass of champagne her way—leaving Gwyn no graceful exit.

"I was just telling Thomas before that a friend of mine once said to me that marriage isn't a success if it lasts, it's a success based on how it lasts," he offers. "Ten or twenty or *thirty-five* good years together is sometimes a stronger statement to make than fifty okay ones together. I believe that."

She nods as though they were in agreement, though of course she knows that he doesn't believe what he is saying—that he has generated this anecdote solely for whenever a friend is in this situation. Gwyn knows him well enough to know that whatever his marriage is really like—and how can anyone outside of it know?—he will never leave it. He believes that staying is the only success. Why shouldn't he? We only believe something else when we have no other choice.

A waiter comes by with a tray of champagne flutes, Gwyn grabbing one as he passes.

"And, of course," Max says, "this is not the best time, but just so you know, Nicole and I would like to buy it. We'd be open to making a generous offer if you'd consider our interest before putting it on the market. As generous as is necessary."

"What are you talking about?"

"The house."

"This house? My house?"

She turns around to look at it across the dooryard, lit up and glowing, against the rain.

"Yes," he says, "your house. Huntington Hall."

They've agreed to table the discussion about the house, she and Thomas, until after tonight. Somehow, figuring out what is to become of the house—letting it go in some way—would make everything final, if it isn't already. It would make it all done.

"It's complicated . . ." Gwyn says.

He interrupts her. "No, I'm sure. I'm just saying that when you two are ready, we are more than ready. My daughter Meredith just had twin boys. And we'd like to get them all out here in

the summers. It will be easier if they have their own place because her husband is such an SOB who doesn't even try to hide
anymore that he hates us." He smiles. "The price we pay."

Gwyn feels her face reddening. She has considered that
Thomas would leave, that he would go to Eve, wherever that
is. And that she would leave too, not wanting to stay here without him. But she hasn't actually considered the house not
being . . . theirs. Only having Hunt Hall be empty? Isn't that
wrong too? And while she could leave it to her children, she
knows—as soon as the thought runs through her head—that
she doesn't want to do that. Thomas won't want that either. At
one point, this house might have seemed like a place for new
beginnings. Now it feels more like a place for letting go of old
ones.

"We can probably work something out," she says.

"Really?" He laughs nervously. "Just like that?"

She turns and looks at her house again. Thirty-five years.
Thirty-five Thanksgiving and Christmas Eve dinners and
Christmas mornings here. Thirty-five Fourth of July parties
and 36 children's birthday parties, 78 overly long visits from
her family. One hundred times that she decided January was
too terrible here and 250 times that she knew there was nothing more perfect than Montauk at the very end of March. Five
hundred times that she went up to the lighthouse for picnics,
709 times that she brought home fresh flowers from the farm
stand in East Hampton, 840 times that they walked down the
bluffs to the beach. Eleven hundred times they read the Sunday paper by the fireplace, 1,300 times that she watched the
sunset from the porch, 1,900 times that they spent an evening
on the swing by the edge of the cliff.

One time, now, that they are standing before everyone they

know, everyone they love, and having a party that is supposed to end with them telling each other good-bye.

She looks in the direction of Thomas, who isn't looking back at her.

"I don't know," she says to Maxwell. "Maybe."

Maggie

She doesn't go upstairs and change. She doesn't fix herself, re-ally. She pulls her hair back in a loose ponytail and walks into the party in her faded jean skirt and pink tank top—her purple bra a little too obvious beneath it. She left her backpack at the Buckleys', with Eve, who was trying to get ready for the wine toast, the cutting of the cake. Still. If she wants to be putting on her best face for this, she certainly isn't. She just wants to get to Nate while she can still remember that part of her does want that, before it feels too late.

The rain is coming down now, unapologetically, the wind whipping into low currents, fighting the outside of the barn, pushing on it. Maggie is wet by the time she enters—water droplets on her arms, her neck—and there is dirt and blades of grass on her feet, where her flip-flops left her exposed.

From the doorway, the barn looks incredible: a shiny, warm refuge from the storm, lit up and bright, the party full of that energy that the best parties have, that intangible quality that means a night has the chance to be memorable, magical. Look-ing around, it's easy to forget what these people came for. It's easy to wonder if they've all decided to forget too.

Maggie sees Nate in the corner of the barn, Nate in a tan suit, orange Converse sneakers on his feet. He looks great. He looks like himself. And she forgets about the rest of it, for a second. She feels so relieved to see him—that she has chosen to see him—that it takes her a second to realize he is standing next to Murph, in her deep skin-colored dress, looking, from here, like one long leg.

She cracks her knuckles and starts to head toward him, toward both of them. Only someone stops her. Thomas stops her. He is talking to a young couple whom he looks less than happy to be talking to. They could be Maggie's age, maybe a little older.

"Maggie," he says, shifting his hand from her arm to the small of her back. "I was just looking for you. This is Belinda and Carl Fisher, who just moved into a house down the road. This is Nate's fiancée, Maggie Mackenzie."

Belinda looks her up and down—her face almost not breaking rank, almost not showing what she is certainly thinking about what Maggie is wearing. "It's nice to meet you. We've heard so much about you."

Like what? she wants to ask, but instead she tries to cover herself, crossing her arms in front of her chest. "You too," she says.

She feels Thomas's hand on her shoulder. "If you'll excuse us, Belinda, I just need a minute with my daughter-in-law," Thomas says, and steers her to the side of the barn, away from the terrible Fishers and everyone else.

"You need a minute away?" Maggie whispers to him.

He shoves his hands deep into his suit pockets, looking exactly like Nate—awkward in this setting, awkward in a way that he won't be able to shed until he is out of his suit, out of tonight's game.

"Is it that obvious? Sorry about that. I'm not a big one for cocktail parties," he says. "Never have been. But Gwyn is great at them."

Maggie smiles. He isn't saying this rudely, but with something like admiration. Admiration that Gwyn is able to stay comfortable in her own skin, or able to fake it better at least.

"Have you been in the house?" he asks, and hands her some cocktail napkins, and she begins drying herself, begins to pull herself together a little bit.

"I've been next door with the caterer, actually, helping a little," she says. "And hiding a little."

"How was that?"

"The helping or the hiding?"

He laughs. "Either."

"Both were okay, I guess."

And he tries to smile. Only there is something behind the smile that can't be hidden, something that Maggie recognizes almost as soon as she sees it. A loneliness. A complicated one, one that he feels he isn't entitled to.

"I'm supposed to make a speech in a couple of minutes about things ending peacefully, lovingly."

"Do you think that's possible? Things ending peacefully?"

"Well . . ." he says. "I'm starting to think the nicer you try to make things at the end, the worse you actually make them."

"Yeah, I'm not sure I would open with that."

He starts to laugh, and Maggie feels herself warm to him. She likes Thomas. She has this feeling that something is going on, something that she doesn't want to know about, but she likes him anyway. Because she can see it: the parts of him—and not just the outside parts—but also the sweetness that he passed on to Nate. There aren't many men who have a real sweetness in them, and there are other things that go with it, but right now, it makes her feel grateful.

"From the little I heard, you and Nate had a tough day around here," he says. "I'm sorry about that."

"Why are you sorry?"

"Because I'm the reason that you are here."

She smiles at him. "Please don't feel badly about that. It's not your fault that things have gotten a little out of hand."

"I wouldn't be so sure of that," he says.

She locks eyes with him and starts to hear something else, something that she has been suspecting—pieces coming together—just as Gwyn walks up to them, looking absolutely stunning in all-white.

"There you are," Gwyn says, looking at Thomas and then noticing her, but with no judgment about what she is wearing—just a quick, sincere happiness to see her. And, in that moment, with all the rest of it, she can feel it. How lovely this woman really is.

"How are you doing, Miss Maggie? I feel like with all the chaos I haven't gotten to spend any time with you."

"Good." Maggie says. "I'm fine."

"Definitely?"

She nods. "Definitely."

"Good. Then can I steal Thomas, for just a minute? I'll bring him back, sooner than you want. I just need to steal my husband so we can get this toast over with," she says.

"He is all yours."

Thomas takes Gwyn's hand and smiles back at Maggie, as if to say, *we'll talk more later, okay?* And she smiles back at both of them as they head to a small table by the front door of the barn—the rain behind them, the house behind them—a single bottle of wine on it, two glasses.

Then she feels someone's hand on the small of her back, Nate's hand, and she turns to look up at him. Murphy, thankfully, is not with him.

"You stayed," he says.

"I stayed," she says.

And he nods, as if to say, *thank you,* as if to say, *I don't know what that means but I'm glad you're here.*

She nods back. *Me too.*

"Where is Georgia?" she asks.

"I'm right here." Maggie turns as Georgia walks up next to her—looking sweet but a little uncomfortable in her halter dress—a half-eaten prosciutto-wrapped asparagus spear in one of her hands. She drapes her free arm over Maggie's shoulder, taking another bite. "These things are totally delicious," she says.

"That is the nicest thing you could have said to me," she says, and pulls Georgia's forearm tighter around her shoulder.

"Really?" Georgia looks at the spear, slightly confused, reaching across Maggie to hand Nate the uneaten bite. "Well, the nicest thing you could say to me is nothing."

Maggie bites on her lower lip, obliging, and turns toward Nate, who is popping the rest into his mouth. "No Denis?" she mouths to him.

He shakes his head, swallowing. "No Denis."

And before she can ask about the rest of it—or not ask about the rest of it—someone is clinking a spoon against a glass, other people chiming in, until mostly everyone is facing toward the small table where Gwyn and Thomas are standing. Maggie looks around at all of them, all of these people who have comprised her future in-laws' life together, all of them with a story to tell about who Gwyn and Thomas have been, who they think they are now. At first it makes her think that this is like a wedding—when else do you have everyone who matters to you both in one room?—but then she takes in the nervous smiles and dazed looks, looks not exactly of approval or compassion but of doubt and anxiety. Doubt that they can escape this same end, anxiety that they won't.

Maggie turns her attention back to Thomas and Gwyn as Thomas starts to open the tall bottle of wine, with a dime-store corkscrew. He is being careful with it, too careful with it—the corkscrew, the bottle—everything starting to move in a rhythmic slow motion as he finally pours Gwyn a glass of the wine and pours himself one too.

As everyone moves closer, Gwyn takes the glass from him, swapping him for a folded piece of paper, which he opens, putting his free palm on her hip. It is like a dance the way they move together, seamless—and totally natural, even now. And so, even in this strange instance, where, apparently, they are about to toast to the end of their union, Maggie is struck all over again by how they look together. They look right.

And then Thomas starts to speak.

"Thank you all for being here tonight, with us, and with our family." He looks at Nate, Georgia and Maggie, and then over at Gwyn, who is looking right back at him. "When Gwyn first suggested doing this, I thought it sounded a little . . . off the wall. Especially for us. Except the closer we've gotten to tonight, the more I've come to understand that tonight is a good thing. It's a way for us to explain that this relationship has mattered. That nothing has mattered more. Even if it is ending now."

Gwyn takes out another copy of the poem, putting her own

wineglass down. "This poem we're going to read is called 'The Empress of Nowhere,'" she says, more to Thomas than to anyone else.

"It doesn't rhyme, so bear with us," he says.

Everyone laughs. This is funny, apparently. Everyone finds this funny. But as they begin to actually read the poem, trading off each stanza, the laughter stops. The laughter stops even though it is a bizarre and very funny poem about a fisherman eating black licorice on a dock in Florida. About how he doesn't like it at first, finds it too bitter, but learns to like it. He learns to like it—not just tell himself he likes it, but truly like it—just in time to realize that there is no more to be eaten.

Maybe the laughter stops because no one understands. You'd have to stretch the poem to make it relevant. You'd have to stretch the poem beyond recognition, as far as Maggie can tell, to have it make any sense in terms of Thomas and Gwyn—and they're offering no explanation about what it means to them, what it might have meant. And she can't help but wonder if she missed something while she was over at the Buckleys', something that would explain why Thomas and Gwyn are choosing to read this.

Only when she looks back and forth between Georgia's and Nate's blank faces, she realizes that they don't have a clue either. No one does, apparently. No one but Thomas and Gwyn, that is, who are red faced and happy, looking right at each other and smiling, really smiling, which all of a sudden seems like the saddest part. It makes Maggie sad to see it so plainly before her. You have something between you after a while, this soft little bug of a thing, its own life form, even if you decide you don't want it anymore, even when you decide you want other things instead.

Georgia crosses her arms over her stomach, clutching the top of her belly. "Wow! They've officially lost it," she says.

Maggie looks back at Gwyn and Thomas still watching each other. It isn't such a great distance. It isn't such a great distance to get to the worst place. And she turns toward Nate, even though she doesn't want to. Even though she wishes that the person she loves most hadn't put them in a position where the distance to somewhere irreversible feels shorter now, where everything feels so hard. But maybe it just is. For now. And maybe the best thing she can do is just to let it be.

She reaches for Nate's hand, holds on to it. "Let's go somewhere," she whispers.

But he doesn't hear her. "What?" he says.

"I want to go," she repeats.

"Let's go, then," he says.

And he starts to pull her out of the crowd, away from here. But before they can get out, Gwyn starts to speak again, and Maggie turns back. Maggie turns back, which may be the first mistake because she can hear it, something breaking in Gwyn's voice. She hears something, impossible, starting to break.

"This is the way we spent our first night together, in a way. And in celebration of that, and everything that has come since, we hope you will raise your glasses and join us in a toast as we cut the cake."

But there is no cake yet. Which is when Eve starts to wheel it in.

And Gwyn says: "Please join us for this one last thing."

Gwyn

This one last thing. Her words are drowned out by the thunder. Gwyn almost can't hear herself, her voice sounding bizarrely far away, displaced, like she has just gotten off a plane, her ears popping, creating a remove she didn't expect but feels relieved to have. It helps her keep going. To the part that is coming next.

In a minute, the cake will be front and center. The red velvet cake. There is only enough cake to serve to ten people, or—maybe the way these women eat frosted carbohydrates— all two hundred guests. There is only one person this cake is really for, though. It is the cake he loves best, and the last time she will ever make it for him. This holy man. Holy and unholy. Right and wrong. Good and evil. Is anything that clear-cut? That able to be separated? If it was, it would be easier. It would be easier to avoid being fooled and confused by the people who hurt us. We could recognize the injuries before they came. We could recognize the places where we will never be safe.

The rain sounds like it is going to break through the barn without any problem at all. Hard, deep raindrops. Breaking only for the claps of thunder. Breaking only for the lightning. Shocks running through her each time.

There are things Gwyn knows. She is holding a poem in her hand. She is looking out at her children, and Maggie—at all of Thomas's and her friends. The ones she likes, the ones she doesn't particularly. They will try to be there for her, on the other side of this, all of them. She knows this. But she also thought she knew something else. She thought there wouldn't be another side of this. She thought she could count on Thomas. She never thought they would actually reach this moment.

But Gwyn turns and sees her wheeling the cake in, in a red chef jacket, matching, almost as though she has planned it, the inside of the beautiful cake. Gwyn is looking at the cake so intensely—the red creeping out beneath the white—that it takes her a minute to meet Eve's eyes, and she almost misses it—almost misses it taking place, the moment that Thomas notices Eve. But Gwyn remembers. She remembers just as Thomas and Eve lock eyes on each other: Eve picking up the cake, holding it in her hands.

They are still there, in that place couples are in at the beginning, in that space where they are so happy to see each other. Surprised and in awe. It is you. I can't believe it. I can't believe you weren't just a dream. So it takes Thomas a moment to catch the rest of it—what it means that Eve is there. What that means that Gwyn has found out.

Her husband turns toward her, his eyes open wide, and Gwyn braces herself against it—her natural inclination to support him, to offer herself to him. She looks hard right back at him so that he knows—without a doubt—that she knows everything. She knows the lies he has told, about where he has been these last nine months, about where he is hoping to go now. Without her.

"Gwyn . . ." Thomas whispers. "Just, please. Let me explain."

Let me explain? This is the best he can say in this moment? This is the best he can offer? What three words could be worse? She can't think of any. She can't think of any that are less appealing, more useless, than these, promising an excuse for the inexcusable.

Let me explain. Like: *let it go.* This is the job. To forgive. To understand. To be generous. Someone else can do that, thank you.

Eve is standing there with the cake. Gwyn looks at her, and then down at her cart, takes the heavy knife from it.

She holds it out to her husband. "Cut the cake, Thomas," she says.

He shakes his head, refusing to take it. She holds it closer to him, her heart beating in her hands.

"Do it," she says.

"I'm not going to do it, Gwyn," he says.

She is aware that they are talking about something other than what they are talking about, but she isn't sure that he knows exactly what.

"Yes," she says. "You are."

Everyone is quiet. She can see them, watching, wondering what is happening. She isn't sure either. She isn't sure what she is actually asking him to do. She just knows that he isn't doing it. He's not doing anything else either. He's not doing what she needs. His hands are by his sides, and he is completely still— the way he has been, forcing her to move around him to get anywhere.

Then she sees it. He glances at Eve. Because it is her that he is most concerned with. It is her that he wants to make sure is okay. First and foremost. Someone is always first. Eve, with her eyes cast down at the ground, is first for him.

And it drops out of Gwyn.

Her last bit of hope.

The hope she didn't fully know she was still holding on to: that confronted in front of their friends, in front of everyone, Thomas would see what he was doing to them, to himself. And that he would turn away from this old fool he is becoming: someone who throws a life away because he is scared. He is scared he is getting too close to the end of his.

Is it as simple as that? All of a sudden it doesn't feel much more complicated. All of a sudden, it doesn't matter anymore.

She looks over at the cake in Eve's hand and imagines throwing it at Thomas. But she can throw the cake or not throw it, and he is still going away. He is still never going to make it okay for her: these two million painful decisions he's made, every lie he's told, every indignity, every injury at her expense, every bit of strength that she has had to conjure up in order to handle this alone, every one of her own mistakes, every piece of her that wishes she'd never end up here. Thomas is never going to make right the hard, miserable fact that even if she knew it was all going to end here, Gwyn would have chosen him anyway. She would have chosen their life, and spent all of it trying to change his mind.

The only thing that is going to make any of that okay is Gwyn doing something else.

Which is when a final, bright belt of lightning illuminates the doorway of the barn, and the driveway outside. Absolutely brilliant, blinding light, momentarily breaking apart the sky.

It is so beautiful and sure of itself, the crack of thunder so immediate, that it takes a second to understand that it has hit the top of a tree—the tallest tree, wide and solid—about ten feet from the front door of the house. It hits the tree, and the tree starts shaking in place, shaking and stuttering—tilting left, first, then tilting right—and then it breaks, the top half of it, flying forward.

Breaking through the roof. Sharp and clean. Less like a crash and more like a cut. An incision. Through the roof and down into the second floor of the house.

The tree embedded there, like it belongs.

Everyone looks at it, the broken tree, in its new resting place. And now it is truly silent. Gwyn can feel it in her chest. Her heart. She can feel it pushing its way out, against her corseting, against the tight material, absolutely unequal to the task. She starts counting windows, trying to figure out where it has landed. From here it looks like the upstairs hallway. But it could be her bedroom. Thomas's and her bedroom. From here, it looks like, when she goes inside, she may very well find the heavy tree on top of their bed.

But, as if it were the most normal thing in the world, Gwyn runs the back of her fingers gently across her forehead.

She doesn't look at Thomas. She is done looking at Thomas. In the periphery of her eye, she can make out Eve still holding the cake. It is hers now. Gwyn picks up her glass of wine and tilts it in her guests' direction, in a final toast. "Thank you for coming," she says.

Then she takes a sip, which is lovely and sweet, but which doesn't at all remind her of the first time she drank it. It could be any wine, it could be any person she first shared it with, any person she was sharing it with now.

This feels like its own kind of hope.

So she takes them with her—the bottle, her glass. She takes them with her, and starts to walk out of the barn, into the rain, and toward her newly broken house.

part four *parting gifts*

Never, never, never could one conceive what love is beforehand, never.
—D. H. Lawrence, after meeting his future wife

Maggie

There is a tree in the middle of the house.

No one is hurt, which feels like the biggest thing, until no one is hurt, and then the biggest thing is that there is a tree in the middle of the house. It has broken all the way through the roof, through the top floor of the house, down the center staircase, like the end of a hundred promises, like the end of whatever had been holding the place up before.

It has cut the house down the middle, or at least from Maggie's angle, it seems to have cut the house down the middle. She stands looking up at it from the bottom of the staircase—its branches coming down the steps, its leaves at her feet.

Everything in here is still frozen. And outside—what just happened outside—feels far away. There was something remarkable about two hundred people stunned silent. Stunned silent, and still. Something grave and impressive about all those people watching in wide-eyed horror as things ceremoniously fell apart.

After the tree hit, no one knew what to do. Most people departed, moving quickly back to their cars—those who could get to their cars. Others hitched a ride with people whose cars weren't blocked. But some stuck around in the barn, offering to call for help, offering to help themselves, as if there were anyone who could make things better now.

She saw one very short man who was particularly upset, talking about how he couldn't believe that this was happening to *his* house. He was searching frantically for Gwyn.

"I'm still interested," he said, when he found her. "But less so."

"That's shocking," Gwyn said, walking away from him.

Now, Gwyn is gone. Gwyn and Thomas and Georgia.

It scared Georgia. Watching the tree hit her house, break it in two. It scared her enough that she felt something move around inside of her—felt something wrong and hard jump inside of herself—and despite Thomas's assurances that she was fine, that she had nothing to be worried about, they are currently driving down into town, through town, to the hospital—to the emergency room, and a doctor who can hook her up to a machine and guarantee her that everything is fine.

The three of them heading to the hospital. In Eve's van.

Georgia and Gwyn and Thomas in the van. Because it wasn't blocked in. Because the Volvos were beyond blocked in. But Eve's vine van was by itself over at the Buckleys'.

And Nate is walking around on the roof. Like a crazy person. Like it is something he knows how to do: trying to measure the damage, trying to measure whether the tree will stay still or sink deeper into the house before the morning, putting them at further risk.

And Maggie is alone again.

In this house, alone again, but this time with the tree.

The rain has stopped. Still, she is half expecting Nate to slip up there, and to come falling down through the branches. To

ride the trunk downward, like a too-long slide. Barring that un-
fortunate outcome, she is feeling too outside of herself—too much
like she is watching her life as opposed to living inside of it—to
figure out what happens next. In a general sense, and in a less
general one. They will probably not be able to sleep here tonight. How could they? And yet, if not tomorrow, soon they'll
have to leave here. Not just Nate and her. But the rest of his
family. They won't be able to do anything here anymore unless
they try to fix this place, and something tells Maggie that fixing
anything here is the last thing on anyone's mind.

She hears someone behind her. She hears the footsteps behind her, and turns to see a handsome guy, a little too baby-
faced for his own good. He is carrying a duffel bag and a guitar
case, and his hand is poorly wrapped in a thick Ace bandage.

And he is, maybe, seven feet tall. From where Maggie stands
he looks not unlike the tree.

"Hello," he says.

"Hello there."

He doesn't look at her. He is looking up at the tree, turning
his head to the side, as if staring at a tree from a different angle
would help it make any more sense.

"Quite a mess someone has made here, isn't it?" he says.

"You could say that."

"I just did."

She looks at him, confused and embarrassed for some reason. She feels, more than anything, a little embarrassed. "Can I
help you with something?" she asks.

"I'm looking for Georgia, actually," he says, which is when
she notices it. The French accent. Georgia's name made to
sound like a slumber party. *Zoor-zsa.* I'm looking for Zoor-zsa.

"Denis?"

He is silent.

"You're Denis?"

He gives her a small wave, only he is still staring up. He puts his stuff down at his feet and keeps looking up at the tree. He doesn't ask her who she is, which Maggie guesses means he doesn't care.

But then he smiles at her, a big round smile that makes his cheeks puff out, bloat, and it reveals a crooked tooth in his mouth—which, Maggie thinks, may be the best part of him.

"You're Maggie. The food writer."

"Former food writer."

He nods. "Former, of course," he says. "It is nice to finally meet you. We've got a photograph of you in our living room, on top of the fireplace. On the shelf that Nate built. It's of you and Nate standing under a tree at some vineyard, holding wine-glasses. You look a lot better in person, if you don't mind my saying so. Less, what are the words . . . washed out?"

She feels herself start to laugh, in spite of herself. "Thanks," she says. "I think."

"No problem."

He rubs his hands together and heads to the staircase, starts bouncing up and down on the lower steps, pulling on the railing with a tight fist, leaves flying around from the impact.

"What are you doing?"

"Checking the endurance."

Checking the endurance? "Maybe I'm a little slow here, but what does that mean?"

"It means the tree is stuck where it is. You don't have to worry. It's fallen as much as it is going to fall. It will stay where it is until someone gets here and does something else with it."

"How do you know that?"

"How do you not?" he says.

She looks at him, confused, this guy who came out of no-where, just like Georgia was hoping he would, just like Georgia would be thrilled to see he has, if she wasn't currently on a strange ride with her parents.

He steps down so he is eye to eye with Maggie. "I guess I missed the party, then?" he says.

"You could say that."

"So where's my girl, then?"

"That's a little complicated. I don't want you to get upset, there's no reason to get upset, but she's on her way to the hospi-tal with Thomas and Gwyn. Thomas says she is fine, that he's sure she is just a bit rattled from everything. When Nate gets down from the top of the roof, we'll take you there."

His eyes light up. "Nate's on the top of the roof? Right now?" he says.

This was his take-away?

"How about I go and get him? Let him know my opinion about the tree? Afterward he can take me to see Georgia. By then she should be calm enough to welcome me with open arms."

He pats her on the arm, almost like she is his little sister, and starts to head back the way he came. To find Nate. To go on a little adventure with him, jumping around on the badly broken roof.

"You know, no one thought you were coming," she says.

He stops walking. "What's that?"

"No one thought you were coming tonight," she says. "No one thought you were going to show up."

He looks at her, not the least bit offended, giving her a big, slightly aggressive smile.

"Except for Georgia," he says.

"Except for Georgia," she says.

"So apparently she knows something that everyone else doesn't," he says.

"Apparently," Maggie says, because maybe she does.

Maggie feels Denis looking down at her, as if waiting for the next thing she was going to say, the next thing she was going to throw at him. So she pretends she has a right, or permission to say it.

"You're having a girl," she says.

"Excuse me?"

"You're having a little girl," she says.

She can't believe she has said it. She is glad it is out there, though, because she wants to hear an answer. She wants to hear an answer that will convince her—that will convince anyone listening—that people can come through, in their own time, that any love story can end well, even with endless evidence banking up that it is going to end another way.

His whole face breaks open, joyful and full of pride. Real, stand-up-taller pride. "We're having a little girl? Excellent. That is very excellent."

Maggie nods. "It is. It is excellent."

He pauses. "You think Georgia would consider naming her Omaha?"

And then there's that.

Gwyn

They are driving Georgia to the hospital in Eve's van. They are driving Georgia to the hospital in Eve's van because it was the only vehicle they could get out easily, and quickly, all the other ones still blocked in by the people trickling out of the party, only slowly making their way off their property.

Georgia is lying down in the back, and Gwyn is up front with Thomas, who is driving. Georgia seems to be sleeping in the back, which feels like more evidence that she is fine, that she has worked herself up—and nothing more.

Thomas hasn't bothered to change his clothes—neither of them has, making them look especially fancy, especially out of place, in this breaking-down van. She looks at the dashboard, which is covered with painted-on butterflies and socialist bumper stickers, a communist flag sticking to the top, suctioned there by a small cup. She doesn't look at her husband.

Thomas is looking straight ahead too, out the windshield, away from her. She knows that he wants to say something. He is still, after everything, just trying to figure out how.

"I never thought it would get this far," he says, finally. He speaks almost inaudibly. In case Georgia is awake. In case she is listening.

"That's no excuse," she says.

"You would have told me I was making a mistake and tried to convince me to do something else," he says.

"So you lied for you?"

"I lied for both of us."

"How do you figure?"

His whisper gets louder. "You would have told me I was making a mistake and tried to convince me to do something else."

She doesn't say anything.

"I was trying to make it easier, Gwyn," he says.

She turns and looks at his profile, his wide-open eyes. Usually they look innocent to her, and probably will again. But right now they just look cowardly. "Who says it should be easy?"

"I didn't say easy. None of this is easy. I said easier."

"Fine, Thomas, who says it should be easier?"

He looks upset. He looks so upset that she looks away. What is she hoping to accomplish? To make him feel so bad that he stays? That won't make her happy, not for long anyway. Not in a sustainable way. Besides, she learned this lesson a long time ago: just because a man looks upset, just because he is upset, doesn't mean he is going to do anything to correct the situation. For himself, for anyone else.

She turns and looks at her husband, carefully, takes a deep breath in. "You really think you love her," she says.

"I wouldn't be putting us through this if I didn't. I wouldn't be risking everything."

"It wasn't a question, Thomas."

"What is your question?"

She won't ask it. Not after thirty-five years of marriage, thirty-six years since they sat together on her building's roof on Riverside Drive. She won't ask it and sound like a love-struck teenager—even if, at our core, whenever we are asking someone to love us who won't, we are all love-struck teenagers, trying to understand: *Why not me?*

"Will it make you feel better, Gwyn?"

"What?" she says. She doesn't know what he is talking about. She hasn't said anything out loud.

"That I'll be sorry?"

She looks at him, and wonders if he believes that. He should. Because Gwyn can't compete with Eve now. She can't offer him the exact pleasures that go along with the opportunity to be a clean slate, again, everything possible in the eyes of someone new. But Eve—or whoever comes after Eve—can't save him from eventually doing the hard work that comes after that. The work he has never wanted to do, that she has spent the better part of her life trying to protect him from having to do. To jump beyond the impasses, the stuck places, to go deeper with someone. You can do the work to honor what you created, or you don't. But if you don't, you get to the same point with the next person, don't you? You get to the same point, the same questioning, until you push through it. Until you are brave enough to not expect anyone else to see in you what you can't see in yourself.

"Maybe it will all work out for the best," she says.

"Really?"

"No."

They are quiet for a moment. Georgia calls to her from the

back. "Mom, I need you! Can you come back here? I can't find my necklace, my horseshoe necklace. The one that Denis got me. Maybe I left it back at the house. But I thought I had it on. And it could be back here. It could be back here somewhere. Can you help me look, please? Because it does that. It falls off."

"Coming," Gwyn says, as she unstraps herself and starts to head to the back of the van, where Georgia is on her back. But Thomas stops her. He reaches out and touches her arm, holds her there on the inside of her elbow.

"I have been studying Buddhism, though," he says. "For whatever it's worth to know that. I've gone on Saturday mornings for silent meditation, and I did go to a retreat upstate. It wasn't as long as I said, but I did go to one. I do feel . . . interested in the teachings."

She has wondered how Thomas is going to get out of the Buddhism thing after the divorce. How was he planning on getting out of that? Post-divorce, telling them he changed his mind? Post-divorce, telling their kids that he now believes in something else? Maybe in the end it won't matter anyway. Maybe it is far easier to forgive your father for being fickle about his beliefs than for being fickle about your mother.

"Thomas, I went to the meditation center in Oyster Bay. I know you haven't been there. I know you have never been there."

"I've been going to a different one."

"A different meditation center?"

He nods.

It takes Gwyn a minute. It takes Gwyn a minute to get to where he is trying to take her. "To the one Eve goes to?"

"To the one Eve goes to, yes," he says.

She looks at her husband, just looks at him. No judgment. "What have you learned, Thomas?" she says. "Tell me one true thing."

He thinks about it, and then he takes his eyes off the road, for a moment, and looks at her.

"We don't know anything," he says. "About what is coming next."

Maggie

Nate is getting ready to take Denis to the hospital. He has changed into jeans and a paint-stained THE HOLD STEADY T-shirt, and is still wearing his orange Converse, which she stares down at when he asks her to come with him, when she tries to figure out why she says no. She decides it is better for her to stay behind for now. She decides—even if the reasons aren't entirely clear to her yet—that she is better off staying in this broken house without him, and if not right away, then soon, surveying the different rooms on the first floor for the worst damage, and using the empty wine boxes to store away what may get lost or damaged.

They are standing on the porch, by the front door, Denis already in the car, ready to get going. Nate looks nervous, shifty, and shifting, from foot to foot. She knows he wants to ask her if she'll be here when he gets back, and feels bad that she isn't making that part easier.

He smiles at her, but she can't make that easier yet either. She can't kick the feeling that something very important has been forgotten.

"Where did you go before? Did you walk all the way into town and change your mind?"

"I didn't even get that far. I ended up next door at the Buck-leys' talking to Eve."

"Eve as in the caterer?"

"Eve as in the caterer."

She pauses, focuses on the word STEADY on his T-shirt before considering whether she is going to say it, before deciding that it really isn't a good idea, and then saying it anyway.

"I think she is having an affair with your dad."

"What?"

He looks like she punched him. That's what he looks like, instinctively stepping back from her. He gives her a stern look, and all of a sudden it feels like he isn't sure he can see her. All day she hasn't been able to see him, and now it is mutual. Maggie isn't sure that this is better, but it surprisingly doesn't feel a whole lot worse.

She puts her hand on his chest, on the STEADY.

"What are you talking about?" he says.

"I'm sorry but there were just things she was saying. And then the way your father has been acting. And maybe I'm par-ticularly sensitive to it today, but I still know what I know. I still *think* I know what I know. Eve said too many things, knew too many things, for me not to start adding it all up."

He shakes his head. "I think you're wrong."

"I don't."

"It just doesn't make sense. You're talking about someone my mother hired to have here tonight. Someone my mother inter-acted with. This is who you're saying my father is involved with?"

Maggie doesn't even have to think about this. She doesn't even have to think if Gwyn knows. Ten minutes with Gwyn, and she knows that Gwyn knows everything: the way so many people do who are underestimated, for a million reasons or one, and therefore have more time to pay close attention.

"Yes," she says.

She makes herself meet Nate's eyes, wondering what he is thinking, wondering if he is mad at her now, too. And maybe he should be, maybe she would be if the situation were reversed. She has no proof about Eve, nothing really close to proof. But maybe being mad—either of them, both of them—isn't so dangerous anymore, and doesn't feel like the thing she should be running from at such incredible speeds. Maybe her fear of anger, and discomfort—both of their fears of that—has contributed to all of this. It has kept them less honest.

She is surprised he hasn't yet asked her: *why is she saying this, why is she telling him right now, even if it is true?*

"Okay, well . . ." he says. "I'll have to think about that."

And maybe they are being honest now, because he does it—what he seemed to be unable to do before. He looks annoyed, really annoyed in a way that seems to indicate that he isn't going to retreat, but step farther in.

"So you'll be here when I get back from the hospital?" he says. "Do I get to ask you that?"

She nods.

"Does that mean I get to ask that or that you'll be here?"

"Either, both."

"Same answer?" he says.

"Same answer," she says.

She knows he needs her to say something, something hopeful, but she isn't sure what to say. And then Denis honks from the car. He honks, in beat, and it takes Maggie a minute to place it, for what it is. A song. A song she can recognize. "Harvest" by Neil Young. The very song she was listening to that morning. What are the odds of such a thing? What are the odds?

"I think that's 'Harvest' he is strumming out there on the horn," she says. "I'm pretty sure. I'm pretty sure that is what is happening."

He looks in the direction of the car. "That's something," he says, raising his eyebrows.

"No, you don't understand. I was listening to it this morning," she says. *This morning* in Red Hook. It feels impossibly far away now. And yet it's not, is it? If she can still remember the song she was listening to, it's only as far away as she decides it needs to be.

Nate reaches out and touches her cheek, first with the outside of his fingers, then with the insides. "You listen to it every morning," he says. Then he pauses. "Don't think too much while I'm gone, okay?"

"I was just starting to get somewhere hopeful."

He shakes his head. "Still, that can flip on a dime."

She smiles. "So what should I do instead?"

"Well, you're an excellent cleaner . . ."

She shrugs. "Tell me something I don't know."

He smiles. "I'll be back soon. We'll start today over."

"There's no starting over, Nate," she says.

He starts to walk off the porch, but he turns back, holds her gaze. "So, we'll figure out a way," he says. "To start here."

Gwyn

She stands looking through the small window on the hospital room door at her husband holding her daughter. They are lying on the far bed in the room, the other bed empty. Georgia is not in labor—false or any other kind—but she is too worked up to go home tonight. And really, what home would she go to? There is a tree in the middle of the one Gwyn has to offer her.

Georgia is better off here: Thomas's arms wrapped around her, her head buried in his chest. His suit wrinkled, the jacket still on. He hasn't even thought to take it off, to loosen his tie. But who is focused on what makes sense, on changing clothes, on getting on with it? Thomas isn't. From here, from where Gwyn stands, her husband is focused on only one thing now, keeping Georgia calm.

Gwyn holds a paper tray of watered-down decaf coffees from the hospital cafeteria. They are terrible and too hot, but they would be welcomed by both of them. She is planning to give them the coffee and then head home to get a change of clothes for Georgia. She plans to head home to get Georgia whatever she needs to stay here. Still, she can't seem to make herself move. She stays where she is, doesn't make a move to go in. But maybe she should have. Because, a moment later, as she is still standing there, she feels her presence behind her. Eve.

Gwyn doesn't say anything at first. She leaves it in Eve's court to do whatever she has come here to do.

"I thought we could trade," she says, holding out Gwyn's keys so she can see them, a strange peace offering. "That you'd want your car. I drove it down here for you guys to take home."

Gwyn turns to her, and takes them. "Thank you."

"No problem."

"We left yours in the van. Thomas seemed to think it would be okay. He put them in the glove compartment. I hope he was right to do that."

"He was," Eve says, and goes to stand next to Gwyn by the window—looking in on them. "About that."

"About that," Gwyn repeats.

"How is Georgia doing?"

"She's fine. Just a little shaken up. We would take her home, to what's left of it, but she's probably better off here. So she'll stay here for the night. I'll go home and get her some things, make it comfortable for her."

Eve nods and Gwyn wonders what she sees when she looks at Thomas and Georgia. Does she see her future stepdaughter, who is the same age as she is? Does she think about having her own child with Thomas? Or is she not thinking about any of that—just hoping that he'll look outside, so she can catch his eye, and be sure that, despite tonight, he still loves her?

"She looks peaceful," Eve says.

"Her father has that effect on her."

They are silent, both continuing to look through the glass at the man they share. Even being with Eve out here, she still feels it rising in her—a generosity toward Thomas again. She feels generous as she watches him with their daughter. He loves their daughter. He loves Nate. He even loves Gwyn. He has done the best he thinks he could for her, for as long as he could for her. Now he is going to go do something else. He has given himself permission.

She turns and looks at Eve. "The storm's over?"

"Yes," Eve says, a little enthusiastically. A little too happy to offer some good news. "It's dry as can be outside, almost like nothing ever happened."

"Except I have a tree through my roof to prove that it did."

"As if you need proof," she says.

"As if I need the proof," Gwyn says, and smiles. In spite of herself.

Eve smiles too, and it lights her face up, almost makes her pretty. Not quite, but almost. When Thomas starts retreating from Eve years from now—when she gives up on him and heads back to Big Sur—she smiles at him in this exact way, but he has a different thought than Gwyn has now, or at least, he names it to himself in a different way. He thinks, *just leave*. He will tell Gwyn this, and she will laugh because they are friends by then. And because she knows Thomas misses her, misses telling her things, and just misses her. He never abjectly notes that he made the greatest error of his life in leaving her, in how he left her, but after Eve is gone, Gwyn knows he will wonder if this is true. Even if it is too late for him to do anything about it. Even if it is too late to even admit, fully to himself, the cost of it. Who can ever admit that, Gwyn wonders? Probably someone who wouldn't have left in the first place.

Only right now, Eve is still in front of her, present. More than present. And she is waiting for something more from Gwyn. This is her own fault, Gwyn thinks, for the shared smile—for the joke. It has probably made Eve think that things are about to go another way.

"I really do love him, Gwyn," she says.

"Excuse me?"

"Tommy. I love him. I love him more than I've ever loved anyone, for whatever that is worth."

Gwyn reaches for the doorknob, her hand starting to turn it. This could go one of two ways. At the end of the day, how big of a person is anyone really supposed to be? "Not a lot," she says.

"Fair enough," Eve says, and gives her a final, sad smile, and starts to walk away.

She starts to walk away, out toward her vine van to wait at home for Thomas's call, to listen as he says he isn't coming to her tonight, but he's coming tomorrow. He's coming soon.

Gwyn clears her throat, turns to look at Eve's retreating back. "But thank you," she says.

"For what?" she asks.

"For tonight," she says. "For doing such a nice job. The food was great. Everyone thought so."

Eve smiles. "Thank you for saying so, Gwyn."

"Well, someone needed to," Gwyn says. "And all that the rest of them will remember now is the tree."

"And maybe the cake."

She smiles. "And maybe the cake."

Then she turns the doorknob, leaving Eve behind, and goes inside to her family, for tonight, while it is still hers.

Maggie

Maggie is sitting on the swing, by the edge of the cliff, smoking. She is smoking too many of Eve's cigarettes. The last time she had a cigarette was during the U-Haul drive from California to New York. Before that, it had been a long time. But during that trip east, when they'd stop at roadside diners, they'd share triple-decker BLTs and sweet iced coffee and one cigarette before getting back in the truck, trying to drive through the night. *We're done with these things when we get to New York,* she remembers telling him. Now she is having several and not thinking about it, except to decide whether she is having another. She is deciding to make the next one her last, and is looking out at the ocean, and trying not to think about anything else too much, except for how long she has been out here, which seems long. Too long, already. She should be inside, helping to do something.

She reaches into her pocket to light the final cigarette, and drops her lighter beneath the swing's seat. She leans down to pick it up, and something underneath the swing catches her eye—writing engraved on the swing's underside. On a metal plate screwed into the swing's underside. It is hard to make the words out in the darkness, but she flicks the lighter open and tries.

She thinks it is a poem, at first, but then she realizes it is a song. The lyrics to a beautiful song, a song she recognizes. She runs her fingers along one of the stanzas:

And you shall take me strongly
In your arms again
And I will not remember
That I ever felt the pain.

She holds her fingers there, over the words. There is something in them that hits her. It hits her now, when she needs it to most, something about belief. She doesn't know how she and Nate will get through this, but she also knows that she believes in him. How can that be? Maybe because, in the end, belief isn't supposed to make sense, at least not all of the time. In that, it finds its power. It gets to creep up on you and carry you forward. Until you can carry yourself again.

She pulls her hand away. She has heard the song before. She can't remember who sang it (it's on the tip of her tongue . . . why can't she remember?) but she starts humming the melody. It is coming back to her a little at a time—the melody—which isn't the worst way to begin to remember the rest.

And she hears footsteps. She looks up, from beneath the swing, thinking it is going to be Nate, coming back for something, but it is Gwyn, walking quickly toward her—out of her dress, and in a pair of jeans and a short-sleeved button-down top.

"You're back?"

She smiles. "I just came back to the house to change, and I got some overnight clothes for Georgia, pack her up a suitcase."

"She's staying at the hospital?"

She nods. "She's okay, though. Just a little wound up. Denis just got there, right as I was leaving, and he is going to stay with her. Thank goodness for that at least. And Nate went to get us all rooms at the inn on Second House Road. But he should be back soon. He wanted me to tell you that he'd be back soon."

She is quiet, not eager to think about Nate coming back, about going to the inn with him or staying here. About anything they have to talk about. Sleep, all of a sudden, seems so far away.

Gwyn sits down on the swing, beside her.

"Are those yours?" she says, and points at the pack of cigarettes in Maggie's hand. "Please tell me you don't smoke."

Maggie didn't remember she was holding them, and immediately gets embarrassed and starts to explain—*not usually, just tonight*—but then she looks back at Gwyn, who is holding her hand out for one.

"Of course not," Maggie says, and hands one over.

Gwyn lights it up, taking a long drag, closing her eyes against it. Maggie watches her, considers telling her that they are Eve's cigarettes she is smoking. Would it matter to her? It seems beside the point. If Maggie is right about Eve and Thomas, or, if she is wrong, it will come out soon enough, and either way these cigarettes are not part of the story.

Maggie points back in the direction of the house. "I'm planning to head back inside and to pack some things up for you guys. Like the photographs along the staircase? Things that seem like they might get waterlogged. If it starts to rain again."

Gwyn nods. "Thank you for that."

"Well, maybe you should see what I've managed to do before you actually thank me. I am terrible at cleaning."

"It gets easier."

"Maybe. But I was standing in the library for less than ten minutes when I saw the swing through the window and decided I had to come out here instead. I had to take a break."

Gwyn picks her feet up, so the swing swings. "You just described every morning for me."

Maggie laughs and runs her hand along the swing's seat, along the wooden boards. "So did Thomas build this?"

"No. Thomas's parents. A long time ago. It was their wedding present for us, actually."

"Champ and Anna?"

"Champ and Anna." She smiles.

"What were they like?"

Gwyn smiles. "Wonderful, really. Very lovely people who liked each other a lot. Anna didn't particularly like me, though. But Champ did. I made him laugh."

"Why didn't she like you?"

"Mother-in-laws are the worst. You know, they don't like you, they make you feel bad about yourself, they have a divorce party the day you meet them and you have to face the fact that they are crazy. Plus, if you aren't very sure of yourself, you may start feeling like you are going that way too."

Maggie smiles.

"I wished you could have met them. You would have liked them. They moved here, for good, after the hurricane of 1938. Anna said Champ was like a man obsessed with Montauk for a while after that. He built the town a library, and helped remake a new town center."

"And then what?"

"And then it calmed down. But he was peaceful here. He was really peaceful." She shakes her head. "I think I thought that Thomas was like him. It was important to me. But being absent and being peaceful are two different things. They can look alike, but they are really the opposite."

Maggie is quiet, thinking about that, hoping that Nate is closer to the second, believing he is. "When did they die? Champ and Anna? I mean I know it was before Nate was born, but—"

"Anna got sick not long after we got married. And the doctors couldn't really do anything to stop it. I don't think Champ could take it without her. He died six months after she did." She takes a final drag of her cigarette. "But they lived a happy life together. Not long enough, but very happy. I think that is better than the other way around."

"How do you get there?" Maggie asks, turning and meeting Gwyn's eyes. "The happy part?"

Gwyn smiles. "You get lucky."

"That's what you've got for me?"

"I'll work on it, and get you something else when I'm a little less tired." She pauses. "Avoiding smoking is probably a good starting point."

Maggie puts her cigarette out on the bottom of her flip-flop, and looks over at Gwyn. "Sounds good."

Gwyn stands up and Maggie can feel her look down at her—carefully—as though she were trying to figure out whether she should say it, whatever it is that she has already decided she needs to say.

"I know you're upset with Nate, Maggie, and who am I to tell you that you shouldn't be? Maybe you should get out now. Maybe when things start to show that they aren't what we think, we are better off hitching ourselves to a different star."

"Really?"

Gwyn puts her hands on her hips, shrugs. "Who am I to know? But I have been thinking a lot today, and for whatever it is worth, there are different ways to have trouble. There are different ways to be confused about how someone's disappointed you. My husband lied about the future because he wanted to forget the past. But Nate lied about the past because he thought it would give you two a future. Don't confuse the two things."

"I couldn't even if I wanted to."

Gwyn reaches over and, without asking, gently takes the pack of cigarettes from Maggie's hands. "What I'm trying to say is that it will be okay between you and Nate. Because you both want that. Because you both want that more than anything. It sounds simple, but I'm learning that the problems start when you want different things."

"Like Mr. Huntington wanting to become a Buddhist?"

"Like Mr. Huntington not wanting to be with me."

Maggie looks down, gets quiet. Her eyes focusing on Eve's cigarette, on what she thinks she knows about Eve, on wondering what the truth of it may be doing to Gwyn, may do to her from now on.

Which is when she remembers—an answer popping into her mind. "It's 'Sweet Thing,' right? It's 'Sweet Thing' from *Astral Weeks*. That would have made me crazy, if I didn't remember," she says, the whole song from under the swing coming back to her. "And there's a great story behind it, why he decided to write it. It's the only song on the album that's about looking forward as opposed to looking back."

"What are you talking about?"

"The song," she says. "The song under the swing."

Gwyn shakes her head as though she had no idea what

Maggie is talking about, and whether she does or not, Maggie can see it: how tired she is. Like Maggie. Maybe more than Maggie. She is too tired to discuss this.

"You know, I'll show you tomorrow," she says.

Gwyn smiles. Then, as if thinking better of it, and doing it anyway, she bends down and kisses Maggie on the cheek.

"It is nice meeting you, Maggie Mackenzie."

"It is nice meeting you too, Gwyn."

Maggie watches Gwyn walk away, waits for the car ignition to start, and then taking a deep breath, she gets up herself, gets off the swing, planning to head back to the house.

But instead of going back to the house, she takes the steep fifty steps down to the beach, the rocks meeting her at the bottom, giving way to smooth sand, giving way to the ocean—right there, suddenly right there—for her to step into.

She slides off her flip-flops and walks into the midnight water, flinching as it freezes around her feet, her thighs. She is hoping it will make her feel clearer, but it is only making her colder. Still, she turns and looks back in the direction of the house. She can see it fairly clearly—all the lights on. She can even make out the tree, the injury, still firmly rooted in the strangest place. She keeps looking anyway.

It may not be what she thought she was searching for, but maybe it will turn out to be what she needs. Because safe or unsafe—safe and unsafe—it is starting to feel like it is her home that she is looking at.

Gwyn

There is a moment in every relationship when you see the whole thing. The question is when does the moment come? Is it the first time you see the person and instinctively know that things between you are going to work out, or fail? Is it a moment in the middle when you've experienced a loss—a parent's death, a sickness—and this person gets into bed with you and holds you all night, until you feel guilt, incredible guilt, at any time you ever questioned him? Or is it a moment toward the end, however you get there, when you realize that there is something behind this person's eyes that you were never able to touch, no matter how hard you tried?

You can only guess at it, where things really end, where they really begin, and so Gwyn knows it is possible that she is wrong that it begins and ends and begins again here. That this quiet moment is her moment. Years from now, it just may define to-night for her, or the end of tonight for her, the end of one part of her life, the beginning of another.

It's also possible she'll forget it. It doesn't feel possible now, but that is the thing when you are still in the middle of some-thing. You can't believe the gods or the universe or all the incontrovertible proof to the contrary. This too shall pass. This, too, doesn't get to count for everything.

Gwyn takes a deep breath, standing in the middle of the driveway, looking around herself, listening to all the noise. This is one of the other things she loves about Montauk—one of her small, forgotten things—how loud it gets here after a storm. She can hear the ocean from where she is standing, she can hear people on the street, and she can hear cars all the way down on Old Montauk Highway.

It is enough, in its way, to make her question her instinct. Her gut instinct to go back into her house and take just a few of her things with her. Right now. To pick up a few of her own things that may be getting damaged, things that she needs and loves, and that one day will remind her what she had in this house. To get them now, before it is too late.

But she makes a decision. It isn't the most important decision she'll ever make, maybe even that night, but she decides to ignore what her heart is telling her to do, and not to go back into her house. Not now. Not when she'll find other proof for herself, as if she needs other proof, that there was a family here. That, soon, they will be gone.

Instead, she reaches into her bag, and finds her keys, and takes them out, and goes to get into her car. She gets into the car and turns on the ignition and quickly turns out of her driveway.

She is going to drop off these clothes for her daughter, and she is going to stay with Thomas, for tonight, at the inn on Second House Road, and she is going back to the hospital tomorrow and she is going to do what is needed. For her daughter. But she isn't going into her house tonight. She isn't even going to look at it in her rearview mirror, or consider it at all.

Call it what you want. But soon enough, less than a year from now, or a little more than a year from now—in the brief space of time where it looks like Thomas may actually marry Eve; in the brief space of time right before they sell their house to a young couple from western Massachusetts, the ones who were willing to go into debt to buy it, the ones who want to turn it back into a full-time home—Gwyn takes this car on a road trip out to Oregon, to stay for a while with her sister and the journalist. At least that is her plan, originally. But she stops along the way in a northern Arizona city, where she walks into a hotel barroom and finds a man sitting there, yellow socks peeking out from beneath his dress shoes. She recognizes him in the way we get to recognize the people we are supposed to meet, the ones we have been waiting our whole lives to meet. Does that mean that Gwyn turns out okay, just because she's found someone else, someone who wants to see her? No, not as far as she is concerned. As far as she is concerned, it means she turns out okay because she believes—in that hotel barroom, for the first time in such a long time—that she should be seen. It is a bonus, of course—an immeasurable bonus, *the* immeasurable bonus of her life—that the man with the yellow socks is the one to do it.

And for tonight, at least, she is done. With this house, this piece of her life, the whole damn thing.

She isn't angry. She isn't hopeful. She is simply done. For tonight, Gwyn is done trying to pick up what cannot be saved.

Maggie

Maggie is trying to pick up what can be saved. She is sitting on the living room floor, the half-filled wine box by her side, books and picture frames and candlesticks and vases surrounding her. She has grabbed newspapers from the kitchen, from the recycling bin there, and is beginning to spread them around her—beginning to get ready to wrap everything around her up—when she looks up and sees him standing there in the doorway, leaning against the doorframe, his arms crossed across his chest.

Nate. He looks like he has been standing there for a while, watching her. He is still holding his car keys in his hands, between his fingers.

"You're back?" she says.

"I'm back."

"And what are you doing standing there?"

"I'm pretending."

"Pretending what?"

"That when you'd look up, you'd still be as happy as you usually are to see me. That your face would light up how it does, you know . . ." He uncrosses his arms, motions with the keys in his hands to his own face. "That I'd get to watch you get a little happy."

She takes a closer look at him. "Did I?"

"Half," he says.

She smiles, looking down at her piles, reaching for more newspaper, trying to decide what to use it for. "That's not so good."

"It's not so bad," he says. "I thought I'd be starting at less than that. So maybe we're doing okay."

The newspaper is turning her hands black and yellow, and she turns it over, away from herself, which is when she catches the headline on the top of the page, the headline announcing that today is the anniversary of the hurricane. Sixty-nine years ago today. Sixty-nine years ago. What was happening in this room then, she wonders? How did they come out the other side of it?

Nate walks deeper into the room, toward her, so that he is just a few feet away from her. He doesn't sit down, though. He waits. He waits for her to give him a sign that she wants that.

"Murph told me what she said to you on the bus. It's not true. We never slept together. We never even kissed. Except during some stupid spin-the-bottle round in the fourth grade."

She looks up at him. "Then why did she say it?"

"Because she could."

"She picked a bad day."

"Yes, she picked a bad day," he says. "Maybe that's not the real problem, though."

"What is?"

He shrugs. "Why were we playing spin-the-bottle in fourth grade?"

She starts to laugh, and feels something come loose in herself, or loose enough that she does it, the first thing: she moves some of the books out of the way, so he can sit across from her.

She moves some bad paperback novels, a small hardback, and an aquatic dictionary, the largest book, out of the way. He sits down, cautiously, leaning backward on his hands, looking at her, really looking at her.

"Thank you," he says.

She nods. "You're welcome . . ."

"What are you thinking?" he says.

She looks at him. "Nothing."

"No, not nothing. Tell me."

"Well, right now I'm thinking that you rarely ask me what I'm thinking." She pauses. "And I'm feeling grateful for that. It's a terrible question. There is nowhere good to go from there."

He smiles, and turns briefly toward the window, looking outside, at the night—the outline of the ocean in the distance. "He asked me something today which I keep thinking about. He asked me a question when we were walking back from surfing earlier."

"Your dad?"

He nods his head, turning back to her, a look passing over his face. "It was strange because he didn't sound like himself exactly. He asked if when I look at you I feel rational. He said I shouldn't," he says. "I shouldn't feel rational about you."

"Rational? What does that mean, even?" she says. "Like I should still be a fantasy?"

"I don't know. That's my point." He pauses. "It sounded like he was talking to himself more than to me."

She is quiet. Part of her wants to ask what Nate says now when he is talking to himself, to ask herself the same thing. Somehow that feels like too big a question. Somehow that feels like everything. Besides, who are we to tell ourselves anything about our lives? Who are we to be brave enough to figure out a new way to live them?

"I'm thinking that with enough practice, you can talk yourself into or out of anything," Maggie says.

"What do you mean?"

"I mean that you should be careful what you say," she says. "I think we should both be careful what we say next."

He leans forward, putting his hand over her chest, clutching her there, his fingers digging in. She is aware of his fingers, and that feels upsetting. His touch unsettles her right now, almost as much as it soothes her. But she has to think that it isn't always going to be like this. As he moves closer to her, she knows she doesn't want it to be like this, and he doesn't want that. She knows that he is going to try to do whatever he can do to fix it. And for the first time, so will she.

It might seem that they haven't moved far from where they started—Maggie started her day with Nate, and she is ending it with him. She is staying in the same place. But she is staying in a new way, a deeper one, which she is starting to understand might be the most important move she ever makes.

He starts to speak, his voice catching. He clears it, and takes a second try. "Maggie, I'm not going to disappoint you again," he says.

She looks at him, right into his eyes. They are endless. And she can see that he believes it. She can see that he believes the impossible, which can be a recipe for disappointment, but is also the first step—the absolutely necessary step—to working toward anything that is possible. And stable. And true.

"You will disappoint me."

"No. Not like this."

"How can you know that?"

He shakes his head, and keeps talking. "Look, Maggie, it doesn't matter in the end."

"What doesn't?"

"Even if this feels fairly awful for a while, I'm going to tell you everything. And I'm not going away unless you ask me to." He pauses. "I'm not sure I'm going even then."

"Are restraining order jokes ever funny?" she says.

"No, not usually."

"Okay," she says. "So I won't make one."

Then she rests her forehead against his, can feel him there, his heart beating there, right where he is touching her. It often feels like that, wherever they are touching, that she is reaching something inside of him. Especially now, when she needs it the most, that feels like its own kind of promise.

"Nate," she says, "I keep thinking about that swing outside. I keep thinking a swing like that would be great in front of our restaurant."

"It would be. It would be perfect." He is talking slow. "How about we ask my parents if we can use theirs?"

Maggie looks at him. "You think they'll say yes?" she says.

"I think we've got a good chance, yes," he says. Then he moves closer, putting his mouth against her ear. And he waits. He waits for just a second, before he says it, real low. "Can I tell you something I've never told you before?"

Maggie closes her eyes, a tear falling out, which she brushes away so he doesn't see it, and so she won't miss it, any of it, all of it, the good part, the hard and real part, that may be coming next.

epilogue

Montauk, New York, 1972

Champ

He is working on the swing.

Anna is sitting on the ground close to the edge of the cliff, pretending to look back in the direction of the house, but she is watching Champ out of the corner of her eye. He knows that she thinks he is too old to be lying on his back working on this swing.

He *is* too old. They live in New York City now, for more than a year now, where things are easier on them. They miss the house, though, miss being out here, in a way they don't like to talk about even to each other.

They are back only for a few days for Thomas's wedding. To the woman Gwyn. The woman that Anna thinks is too pretty.

"He doesn't have to look hard enough to find it," she says. "Her beauty."

"So?"

"It's harder to appreciate what you don't have to look hard to find."

They have had this conversation before. Champ focuses on polishing the underside of the swing. It is almost done. It is their wedding present to Thomas and Gwyn. It is their offering.

He rubs his hand along the wood. "They'll be fine, Anna," he says.

"You don't know that."

"No. I guess you can never know that. But I do like her."

"What could be more beside the point?" She turns and looks at him straight on. She is better at this now, saying exactly what she thinks.

And he doesn't say what he thinks because he is better at knowing what she isn't ready to hear: that he has no idea whether it will last for his son and his wife, the way it lasted for him and Anna. It could go either way. It always can go either way, can't it? You can stay together for the wrong reasons as much as for the right ones and who is to say you'll be more or less happy either way? Because of a storm, because her arms were out-stretched . . . Champ only knows that the important part is to decide to stay. Again and again. And, on the days you can't, to resist deciding anything else.

"Read the lyrics to me."

"Again?"

"Again."

The lyrics are engraved on a blue plate beneath the seat. The lyrics to their song—Anna's and his. It hadn't been their wedding song. What had been? A Cole Porter tune, if he's remembering right. "Begin the Beguine." It had been so many people's wedding song that year. But this song became the one they played the most in recent years. It is the song that Champ would put on the record player on the cold winter nights out here, toward the end, when they needed a reminder that they wanted to spend the cold winter nights out here.

Hopefully, it would help hold Thomas and Gwyn during their beginning.

He's screwed the plate to the innermost plank of wood, somewhere you have to look close, somewhere you have to be lucky just to find it. And he doesn't skip any of it this time when he reads the words to her:

> And I will stroll the merry way
> And jump the hedges first
> And I will drink the clear
> Clean waterfall to quench my thirst
> And I shall watch the ferry-boats
> And they'll get high
> On a bluer ocean
> Against tomorrow's sky
> And you shall take me strongly
> In your arms again
> And I will not remember
> That I ever felt the pain.
> And I will raise my hand up
> Into the nighttime sky
> And count the stars
> That are shining in your eyes
> And I'll be satisfied
> Not to read in between the lines
> And I will walk and talk
> In gardens all wet with rain
> And I will never, ever, ever, ever
> Grow so old again.

"It's perfect," Anna says. "It makes me want to go listen to it."

"So we'll go listen. As soon as I finish."

"But we're not going to tell them it's here?"

"No," he says. "They'll find it one day. Or someone will find it."

She smiles. "Like a second gift."

"Like a blessing."

She goes and lies beside him, her husband. "Who are you to bless anyone, old man?"

He laughs, and wonders, for a second, what a stranger would think if he came upon them. Two people lying here, between their home and the rest of everything. Would he know that they spent their whole lives here? Would he know that that has made all the difference? Would that even be the truth?

He looks at his wife, watches as she closes her eyes and takes in the late-day sun.

"Can everything end right here?" she says. "When we get to be this happy?"

He moves closer to her. "It just did."

Author's Note

In early spring 2005, I drove with a friend to Montauk, New York. While heading over the Napeague stretch, my friend mentioned a hurricane had hit this area in the 1930s, which separated Montauk from the rest of Long Island.

I began wondering: whose house could have survived such a powerful storm? What would be happening in that family today?

For their help as I aimed to answer these questions and understand everything about the Hurricane of 1938, I am grateful to Robin Strong and the entire staff at the Montauk Library. Several texts and documentary films were useful in my research as well. In particular: *Sudden Sea* by R. A. Scotti; *The Great Hurricane: 1938* by Cherie Burns; Scott Morris's *From the Ashes: The Life and Times of Tick Hall*; Abianne Prince's *Voices in Time: An Oral History of Montauk 1926–1943*; *A Healing Divorce* by Phil and Barbara Penningroth; and *When Things Fall Apart* by Pema Chodron.

I took liberties in changing facts and playing with pieces of history in order to make my story work the way that I wanted it to work. These were intentional choices.

A final note: For their support as I worked to complete this book, I am indebted to my wonderful editor and agents—Molly B. Barton, Gail Hochman, and Sylvie Rabineau. My gratitude also goes to Gwyn Lurie and Ben Tishler, on each coast, to my family and friends for generously reading many drafts, and to Joe the Art of Coffee and The City Bakery for giving me warm and welcoming places to write them.

And a big thank-you to the many people who shared their personal stories with me while I was working on this book. We all live such quietly brave lives, and I feel blessed that I was invited into yours.

—LD, January 2008

THE DIVORCE PARTY

Laura Dave

An Introduction to
The Divorce Party

Gwyn Huntington knows how to throw a party. And Hunt Hall, her postcard-perfect Victorian home in Montauk at the easternmost tip of Long Island, is no stranger to celebrations. But on the morning of her thirty-fifth wedding anniversary, she's putting finishing touches on the last party she'll host there. The last time she'll see Hunt Hall abuzz with caterers and bartenders. The last time she'll preside over a gathering of beautiful friends chatting in candlelight. The last time she'll fully play the role of Mrs. Thomas Huntington. Divorce parties have become commonplace, if not fashionable, in Montauk. But Gwyn is determined that hers will be different.

Just over one hundred miles away on the same morning, Maggie Mackenzie sits on the floor of her Brooklyn apartment attempting to organize her new life. A former travel writer, she's fallen in love with a wonderful man, gotten engaged, and is planning to start a business with him. Today is also the day she'll meet her fiancé's parents for the first time. She's feeling particularly uneasy about the occasion surrounding her first meeting with Nate's family.

The Divorce Party takes us into the lives of these two women at opposite ends of marriage. For all the differences between them—distance, privilege, age—Gwyn and Maggie have one thing in common: each has found herself at a crossroads. Gwyn has been preparing for this day, the last predictable day before an uncertain future. Even though she's had time to come to terms with her divorce, she still can't quite believe her marriage is over. How can she move on when her marriage has defined who she is for the last thirty-five years? And for Maggie, the emotionally charged trip to Montauk shakes the foundation of her relationship with Nate and dredges up feelings she has spent her life trying to avoid.

In the end, Gwyn and Maggie face the same questions: How hard should you work to stay with the person you love? And when is it time to let go?

A CONVERSATION WITH LAURA DAVE

How did you get the idea for The Divorce Party?

Since I first learned about divorce parties, I have been intrigued by them. On one level, a divorce party makes sense to me as a concept: let's celebrate what we've had, as opposed to letting it end acrimoniously. On another level, I think marital break-ups are difficult for a reason: they are supposed to be. Something sacred between two people has broken down. Yet regardless of how we may personally feel about the idea of divorce parties, they are gaining a phenomenal momentum and I wanted to explore this within the context of one family.

This is the first novel to explore the world of divorce parties. My novel also ended up exploring in equal measure how we build a life with someone and how we keep that life secure.

The setting of the novel plays a big role in the story. Why did you choose Montauk?

I have always been drawn to towns on the end of the earth: fishing towns, cliffside towns, towns with more ocean surrounding them than land. They require something different of their inhabitants. Living in a city there are so many distractions, so many ways to avoid knowing what is really going on inside of you, inside of your closest relationships. The quiet in Montauk—the solitude and isolation there—requires an attention to one's own life that I greatly admire.

I also like the juxtaposition of people who live in Montauk year-round and the summer people, who come in and try to take over for a while. There seems to be a reclaiming that occurs perennially—an acknowledgment each September that *this place is ours*—which is incredible to witness. That type of devotion to one's home isn't unlike what is necessary to keep a marriage strong or to keep a family together.

What prompted you to write the novel from two perspectives? Do you think the novel would have been different with a single narrator?

Maggie was originally the sole narrator of *The Divorce Party*. It was going to be, more simply, a story of a woman struggling through the fast and hard realization that the life she was signing up for would be much different than she'd imagined.

But when I began writing a scene with Maggie's mother-in-law Gwyn, my compassion for her was so ardent that I thought, there is something on this side of the story, too. In fact, this is the other side of the same story. To truly understand what it means to sign up for one's own life, we need to consider that despite our best intentions life can fall apart one day. At these very different life stages that Maggie and Gwyn find themselves in, there turn out to be the same difficult questions: What matters most to me and what am I willing to risk? And what, in this life, am I brave enough to fight for?

By following two women at such different points in their marriages, did you hope to explore something specific about marriage or relationships in general?

I am interested in the question of forgiveness. Clearly, being able to truly forgive is necessary in order to stay with one person over the course of a lifetime, and certainly necessary if two people are to remain in love with each other.

I believe that there is no weakness in forgiveness. But we are conditioned these days to think that there is, that the brave thing is to move on when someone disappoints us. It makes it hard to make a relationship work, especially long-term, if the premium is as much on leaving as it is on figuring out a way to stay.

A Buddhist nun, Pema Chödrön, wrote an amazing book called *When Things Fall Apart*, in which she talks about how the only way to stay in a sweat lodge—to experience all of the good and bad it brings—is to not sit near the exit. Because if you are sitting near the exit, you will find a reason to use it. I wanted to explore the idea that to find the joy in your relationship or marriage—to be present for it, to help it grow more sacred— you can't be looking for a way out of it.

Which story was more of a challenge to tell, Maggie's or Gwyn's?

Maggie actually turned out be a harder nut to crack. She didn't know herself very well. Or, I should say, she was in conflict about knowing herself as well as she did. Until her hand was forced about halfway through the narrative, I wasn't sure what she was going to do—when she was going to overreact, when she was going to get mad about the wrong (or right) thing. But once Maggie tapped in to her own culpability in the problems she and Nate were having, she had a new journey. She had to learn to let go of her false notion that someone else was going to magically make the contradictions within her own soul disappear. Maggie is a character who, for very valid reasons, is always going to struggle with wanting to cut and run. Her question becomes am I going to disappear, like usual, or will I figure out a way to fight that impulse?

Do you identify with any one of the characters more than the others?

I identify with so many of the characters, and I want to hug all of them! Especially Thomas. I want to shake him, and then I want to hug him and make some soup for him. But at the end of the day—or the end of today, at least—I think I identify most strongly with Nate. Like Nate, I have been tempted to hit the "begin again" button many times in my life, and I understand all too well his desire to protect the people he loves the most from everything. Even from himself. It is a misplaced desire, and one that gets those of us who have it into heaps of trouble. But there is little doubt that Nate's heart is in the right place.

Were you ever tempted to write a different ending for Gwyn and Thomas?

I am still tempted. I want Gwyn to have everything she wants, and I think there is so much genuine love and affection between Thomas and her. It is heartbreaking. But I also believe that sometimes the universe has more compelling plans for us than we have for ourselves. Having faith in that can be freeing. And I certainly think that is the case for Gwyn, and all that is next for her.

Was the experience of writing this book different from your first, London Is the Best City in America?

Very different, yes. *The Divorce Party* was more difficult because I was dealing with two narrators. I wanted to figure out how their stories were speaking to each other, as well as speaking on their own, and, in the midst of this, I was also dealing with very painful topics. At times I felt subsumed by the stories I was trying to tell. But I couldn't seem to make myself give up, which I am grateful for. Nothing worth having comes easy, right? And now that I've finally come to the end, I feel great pride in this book.

Is it true that The Divorce Party *is being made into a movie?*

I am pleased to say yes! The movie rights to *The Divorce Party* were picked up by Universal Studios for Echo Films, Jennifer Aniston and Kristin Hahn's new production company. I am so excited about that—I think it is going to be a great movie.

What are you working on now?

I am working on my third novel, which takes place in Big Sur, California. It is a story about a thirty-three-year-old woman, and her father, Kyle, who is a former San Francisco 49er, and who raised her alone from the time he was nineteen. This is the only time I've started a book by writing the final scene first. And I'm pretty sure—now that I'm talking about the scene—that I'm going to have to toss it. But while I still have it, I love it.

QUESTIONS FOR DISCUSSION

1. Nate suggests that people with *some* money act differently than people with a *lot* of money. What does he mean? If you were to come into a large sum of money, in what ways would you expect it to change you? How would you want your life to stay the same?

2. Gwyn seems to place most of the blame for her marital problems squarely on her husband. How much responsibility does Eve bear? Do you think Gwyn should have been harder on her? How much responsibility lies with Gwyn?

3. Put yourself in Maggie's shoes. Would your trust in Nate be shattered? Do you think you'd be able to overcome your uncertainty about him? Is it ever best *not* to know the truth?

4. Do you think a divorce party is a good idea? Would you hold a celebration for a divorce or a break-up? Would you attend one?

5. How do you see Gwyn faring? What about her husband's relationship with Eve? How do you expect it to evolve?

6. Should Gwyn have confronted Thomas earlier? How do you think their story would have been different?

7. In what ways has Maggie been affected by her mother's leaving? What about Nate and Georgia? How have they been affected by their relationships with their parents?

8. Do you know women like Murphy? Why do you think she would make up a crazy story and make a stranger uncomfortable? Maggie could have avoided worrying about Murphy if she'd only confronted Nate about what Murphy said. If she'd come right out and asked him, do you think Maggie would have believed Nate's denial?

9. Music is woven throughout *The Divorce Party* and is ultimately critical to the book's resolution. Why is music such an important part of love stories?

For more information about or to order other Penguin Readers Guides, please e-mail the Penguin Marketing Department at reading@us.penguingroup.com or write to us at:

Penguin Books Marketing Dept.
Readers Guides
375 Hudson Street
New York, NY 10014-3657

Please allow 4–6 weeks for delivery.
To access Penguin Readers Guides online, visit the Penguin Group (USA) Inc. Web site at www.penguin.com and www.vpbookclub.com.